The knife of the priest fell, striking into the chest of the victim. Swiftly, with practiced hands, the priest removed the heart of the sacrifice and held it up for the thousands in the streets below. Moctezuma whimpered as he saw what happened next. The sacrifice sat up at the altar, his chest a gaping, draining, ragged wound. The sacrifice reached out his hand, reclaiming his own beating heart from the hand of the priest, and then rose from the altar . . .

D0905726

Charter Books by Barry Sadler

CASCA:

THE CONQUISTADOR

BARRY SADLER   #10

CHARTER BOOKS, NEW YORK

CASCA #10: THE CONQUISTADOR

A Charter Book / published by arrangement with
the author

PRINTING HISTORY
Charter Original / February 1984

All rights reserved.
Copyright © 1984 by Barry Sadler
This book may not be reproduced in whole or in part,
by mimeograph or any other means, without permission.
For information address: The Berkley Publishing Group,
200 Madison Avenue, New York, New York 10016

ISBN: 0-441-09241-1

Charter Books are published by The Berkley Publishing Group,
200 Madison Avenue, New York, New York 10016.
PRINTED IN THE UNITED STATES OF AMERICA

CHAPTER ONE

Castile

Shadows drifted over Sevilla, hiding a thousand evils in its wisps of swirling dampness. Behind shuttered windows, those whom the Spanish Inquisition had branded as heretics prayed for salvation; at the same moment in the dungeons of the Grand Inquisitor, the devout monks of the order granted salvation to the worst of the heretics, sorcerers, and witches by burning them alive in the name of the blessed, gentle, all-merciful Lamb.

The terror was upon Spain. Thomas Torquemada, the Grand Inquisitor who possessed the full blessings of Holy Rome, had the responsibility to purge Spain of all heresy and sedition.

Before he had been summoned to take over the office of Inquisitor, the Dominican monk had been content to serve as the prior of the monastery of Santa Cruz at Segovia. But his learning and devotion had caused Cardinal Mendoza to nominate him for the office. Now he sat at his desk reviewing the new lists of names given to him of persons who possibly were heretics or workers of evil. He pulled back the cowl from his plain wool cassock. He wore his fine red robe only when conducting an official interrogation or trial. He affected no display of wealth or riches. His reward came from the satisfaction of one who has been serving his god to the best of his ability and knows that he has done well. Since February 11, 1482, the date on which His Eminence Sixtus IV, the Holy Father, had appointed him, at the request of Isabella, as Inquisitor General, he had performed his sacred task with single-minded devotion. He had found his calling.

The single candle on his desk cast no softening shadows on the sharp, angular, sixty-five-year-old features. The deep sockets of the man's head housed dark eyes that appeared to have a fire in them of their own and flickered with righteous fervor when he was able to force another heretic to admit his sins. They were so stubborn. He was pleased that he had had to put only a couple of thousand to the burning stakes. Most would readily confess and recant with just a touch of the thumbscrew or boot; the Church could forgive them once they proved their new faith by giving up all their worldly goods, for blessed are the poor.

Not all of his work had gone as he would have chosen. The Moriscos were permitted to live, those unclean blasphemous former members of the Moslem faith. In his heart, he knew that they had no real love for Mother Church. Tens of thousands of them had fled across the straits to north Africa, leaving their lands and goods behind. They should have been burned. And then there were the Jews, who, he felt, celebrated cabalistic rites and black masses and performed vile sorceries. Even now they were being permitted to leave Spain unmolested, taking their goods with them. He was not a foolish man; he well knew that the Inquisition served the purposes not only of the true Church but also of the powers seated upon their thrones. Through the Inquisition, they were able to weed out, and if not kill then neutralize by imprisonment, those they thought not loyal to their thrones. But the Jews had bought their way out for the incredibly small price of thirty thousand gold ducats. Those who had not embraced Christianity, he thought, a hundred and seventy thousand now-lost souls, were being set free upon the rest of the world to work their evil.

Torquemada's old heart pounded, recalling the evening when he had confronted Ferdinand and Isabella, crying to them as he threw his crucifix on their dinner table:

"Will you, my king and queen, do as Judas has done and

betray your Lord for money?'' If they had not been the king and queen of Spain, he would have had them put to the "Question" for their actions.

The blue veins in his wrinkled hands nearly burst with tension as one hand attempted to strangle the other in his passion for justice. His meditations were interrupted by the entrance of Frey Francisco Morella, a good and valued servant of the Lord. The man was still in his twenties and destined for great things in the Church, if his past history of service to the Inquisition was any indication. He entered the office on sandaled feet, his brown homespun robe rustling softly as he approached the Inquisitor General.

"Father, I am sorry to interrupt you at this hour, but we have found something which I think merits your personal attention."

Torquemada leaned back, sucking in a deep breath and releasing it slowly; this helped him regain his composure. Weary as he was, he smiled at his faithful aide.

"What is it, Brother Francisco, that keeps you awake this night?"

Francisco wrung his hands in consternation. "Father, I believe we have found a sorcerer. In all our years, I have never seen one who more surely has the mark of the beast upon him."

Torquemada sucked his lower lip. "Has he been put to the Question?" Even in the pale light of the candle, he could see that Francisco's face was paler than normal, the lips almost white. The brother was deeply disturbed.

"Yes, Father, both the boot and the screw. He admits nothing." Francisco almost broke into sobs, dropping to his knees to grasp the blue-veined hands of his superior.

"Father, you must come and see this creature for yourself. He is beyond my experience, and I confess that I have a great dread whenever I am within the sight of his eyes."

Gently, Torquemada removed his hands from the grasp of his younger servant. "Very well then. I suppose that I must go and see this person you speak of. As we walk, tell me what you know of him."

Guards posted at his door accompanied the good father as they did everywhere; there were heathens hidden, even in the palaces, who wished to stop his sacred work. In front and

behind, the stern-faced soldiers of Catholic Castile escorted
Torquemada and Francisco down the corridors leading to the
dungeons. On the ground floors were fine offices, halls, and
galleries with their walls covered with the work of Spain's
finest artists and sculptors. Rare beauty marked every turning.
But once the great oak door by which two guards stood closed
behind them to let them into the inner regions below the fine
rooms, they entered if not hell then at least purgatory.

The smell of charcoal reached up the several tiers of stairs lit
by lamps in brackets bolted to the stone sides of the walls.
Francisco lent his arm to the Inquisitor as they went down two
levels. On the first level were the cells where lesser offenders
were kept. Below them were the true dungeons and torture
chambers where the servants of God kept an endless vigil, performing their duties around the clock. From sun to sun they
worked in relays, using the thumbscrew and rack or straps and
water. Only the use of iron was forbidden them in the treatment of heretics, but through long practice and study, the loss
of iron was of small importance. They knew how to make up
for its absence.

The peasants swore that they could hear the sounds of
screaming coming from the dungeons at all times of the day
and night. But if it grew too loud, it was said that a block of
wood was forced between the jaws, stopping most of the out-
cries. Those who were returned to their cells were usually too
exhausted to do more than whimper in their sleep.

The dungeon carried in its damp, smoke-streaked stones the
aura of pain. One prisoner caught a quick glimpse of the sharp
profile of Torquemada as he descended to the main chamber.
That one look was enough to cause the man to loose his bladder upon himself, sending him back to the pile of filthy straw
that served as his bed to whimper and pray for mercy from
someone, anyone.

As they neared the bottom steps, Frey Francisco filled in the
details which had brought this new prisoner to their attention.
The man had been arrested by soldiers for riotous behavior in
a tavern well known for its bad reputation, but it was tolerated
on the waterfronts as a necessary evil as long as the evil was
kept within the tavern's own walls. This person had carried a
fight into the streets, mauling several citizens and breaking the
arm of one of the soldiers when he arrested him. During the

confrontation, the man's tunic had been ripped from his body, exposing him to the eyes of the soldiers. They responded in the proper manner once they saw him and took him to the offices of the Inquisition rather than to the jails which housed those with lesser offenses.

"I must warn you, Father," Francisco said nervously to Torquemada, "this man has a most vile aspect in both body and speech. He blasphemes with every other word, and when I tried to offer him solace in the name of Jesus, he told me to take my crucifix and to perform the most abominable rites with it."

At this hour, no one was being put to the Question. Only two jailers and the night warden were to be seen, half dozing as they watched over their charges. When the footsteps of Torquemada and Francisco were heard, the warden came rapidly to his feet, rousing his dozing aides, bowing profusely, eager to serve his master.

"Where is the one who insulted Frey Francisco?" inquired Torquemada gently. The warden in charge of this section of the dungeons bowed and scraped as he led the way to where the new man was being kept.

"He is stoutly chained, Father. For certain, he is a strong brute such as I have seldom seen. If he hadn't been drunk, I don't think even my three good men could have gotten the shackles on him." Torquemada's curiosity was definitely piqued.

Carrying a torch before him, the warden led them to the cell nearest the rack, where the torturers did their best to straighten out the attitudes of the recalcitrant. Unbolting the door, he entered first, making room by standing against the side of the cell to allow his guests more room to view their prize.

The flames of the torch gave the small cell a hellish aspect. Torquemada automatically made the sign of the cross when he saw what the flames of the jailer's torch exposed to his eyes.

Motioning for the jailer to hold his torch over his charge, Torquemada moved a bit closer, covering his nose with a sleeve to keep out the worst of the odors caused by years of men defecating and urinating on the stone floors. The urine had dried and built up in the corners in yellow, weeping, crystalline piles. He inspected the unconscious figure whose

chains had been drawn in, keeping him close to the walls. Torquemada was careful to keep out of range of the powerful
arms and hands.

In all his years, he had never seen a body such as the one
before him. Never had he witnessed a figure so scarred and
gouged that yet had the force of life within its shell. The man
had one long scar that ran from his right eye to the corner of
his mouth and gave him, even while unconscious, a sinister
aspect. To the mind of Torquemada, this man should have
died a dozen times over; that much he knew from his long experience in the service of the Church as Grand Inquisitor. His
duties required a fair knowledge of anatomy and what the
human body could endure before the flesh gave up the spirit.
This thing before him, huddled against the stones of the cell,
should have been dead.

A shiver ran over the muscles of the man's arms, which rippled like the flanks of a horse trying to shake off a nagging fly.
The shiver continued up his body to his face. Torquemada
stepped back as the man's eyes opened, squinting at him
through sticky, swollen lids.

Seeing that the eyes had intelligence in them, Torquemada
addressed the man. "By what name are you called, señor?"
The man attempted to speak but could give only a dry croak.
Torquemada ordered the jailer to give the man water to clear
his throat. Reluctantly the jailer obeyed. He didn't like getting
too close to the man who nearly had broken his jaw with a
wild backhand swing while they were getting the shackles on
him. Torquemada observed the reluctance of the jailer with
contempt. The man was supposed to be capable at his job, yet
he feared a chained man. Taking a clay water jug, the jailer extended his arm to pour the fluid over the prisoner's face.

The scarred man raised his face to the moisture, sucking it
into his mouth. The fluid quickly returned suppleness to dry
membranes.

Torquemada repeated his question. "By what name are you
called, señor?"

With consciousness returning, so did the pain where the
thumbscrew and boot had been applied lovingly to him. They
were simple enough devices in principle, no more than vises
that could be tightened a turn at a time until, if enough turns
were made, the bones would at last crack and then be crushed,

leaving the prisoner crippled for life. This was not the first time he had tested them, and he'd long since learned to put pain in the back of his mind, where he could temporarily ignore it. It was there, but it wasn't so intense. He had known more pain than these people could imagine in their wildest nightmares. There was nothing they could do to him that had not been done already, yet he lived and would live long after their bones had turned to dust.

Casca tried to focus on the thin face above him and bring the sharp features into clarity. When he did, he didn't like what he saw.

Straightening up as best he could against the cell wall, he answered hoarsely, "Who the hell wants to know?"

Torquemada was not shocked that the man did not recognize him; rather, he was offended by the lack of respect in the voice.

"My son, I am a servant of the Lord, a simple priest dedicated to His good works. My name is Father Thomas Torquemada."

For some reason, that news did not surprise Casca; he'd had a premonition of things going from bad to worse when he'd opened his eyes and looked at the harsh face above him, a face he had seen many times. Although the features were different, the fervor of religious fanaticism was clear. He had seen it in the eyes of the priests of Ahura Mazda and those of the Teotec who sacrificed living hearts to their gods. They all performed their sacred and priestly duties, convinced that what they did was best for their victims and their souls.

Casca laughed bitterly. "Yes, good Father, I have heard of the fine work you do. But what am I here for?"

Torquemada smiled gently at his guest; the first steps had been made. One had to get his subject talking to get to the source of things, even if the subject was somewhat rude or disrespectful; he could deal with that.

"You have been brought here to answer some questions, my son, that is all."

Casca shook his head, trying to clear his mind further. "Yes, I have already, as you say, been asked a few things by your associate. He does have a way with words." Casca held up his hands where the pressure of the thumbscrews had swollen them to twice their normal size. Less than ten minutes earlier, they had been three times their normal size.

Torquemada sighed at the weight of his responsibilities. "You know, of course, that the measures taken to get you to speak the truth are approved of and sanctioned by the Holy Church. If you object to them, you object to the Church, and that is heresy."

Casca snorted, cleared his throat, and spat a hunk of phlegm near the foot of the Grand Inquisitor. "What you mean is, damned if you do and damned if you don't."

Torquemada looked at Frey Francisco and nodded his head. He was beginning to understand the problem. The man was definitely most unrepentant for his actions and had a serpent's tongue in his mouth. Yet he had to try again. "All you have to do, my son, is answer our questions and prove that yours is not an evil spirit and therefore hostile to the Church. Even if you have been possessed by some evil, you may confess and recant, and the Church will forgive you and purge you of your sins, thus opening the gates of heaven to your immortal soul."

Casca nearly choked laughing; he couldn't help himself, even though he knew his answers were getting him into ever deeper shit.

"Immortal soul? What do you know of immortality? Look at me, priest. Look closely at me."

Torquemada couldn't resist the compelling quality in the man's voice. He came closer, focusing his brown eyes on the blue-gray ones of the man before him.

Casca lowered his voice to barely more than a whisper, but Torquemada heard every word with startling clarity. "I have seen things of which you have not dreamed of and walked where others would die. I have that which you cannot take from me, though I would give it to you gladly if I could. Look at me!" The cords in his neck stuck out, attempting to burst free from their fleshy shell. "Look at me! I am the death that walks with every man, but I cannot feel it myself. I am the beginning and the end of my own existence. Look at my body! Do you think you can do more to me than has already been done? I have tasted the flames of the stake, and I live. Swords and spears have gone through my body, yet I am alive. I have seen and experienced every perversion and cruelty known to the mind of man, yet I exist and will long after you and the Inquisition have become no more than something for some distant scholar to muse and laugh over, for I knew Jesus as you never could or will!''

Torquemada jerked back, breaking contact with Casca's eyes. He did not doubt that the man, if he was a man, was speaking the absolute truth. He had seen things in his eyes, shadows of things dark and secret. For a moment, he thought he even saw the Blessed Lamb on the cross and the spear being thrust upward into the side of the Son of God. Torquemada, with Frey Francisco beside him, began to pray for the strength to defeat this thing of evil who mocked Him and His holy way.

Casca knew that he had just let his mouth overload his ass, as it had more than once in the past. Now he had no choice but to play it through. He could see the superstitious fear on the faces of the two priests and the jailer. If he was to have any chance, it would be to play on that fear. He gathered all his strength into his voice, the words thundering throughout the dungeons and torture chambers.

''Priests, this I swear to you by all things foul and evil. Burn me and you will set loose with my ashes such as you have not dreamed of. Open my veins and my blood will bring damnation to you. Put me on the rack and I promise you such horror as will shrivel your very soul into a thing of pity and disgust, forever condemned to the deepest pits of hell.''

Torquemada touched his crucifix to his lips at the blasphemy and hate being poured out at him. Frey Francisco was in a state of near panic. Of all the thousands they had put to the Question, never had they come close to anything such as this.

Casca knew that he was close. ''You want proof, then watch!''

He put his forearm in his mouth and began to chew, biting deeply into his own flesh, twisting and tearing till blood ran freely down his mouth into the hairs of his chest over the scars and filth. A deep, ragged tear was opened in his arm. He held it up in front of the priests for them to see.

Torquemada nearly fainted as he watched the blood cease to flow and the wound before his eyes begin to close. Slowly but surely the wound was healing itself as he watched. Casca smiled evilly. ''If you need further proof, touch my blood to your lips and know hell. In the blood of Jesus is life; in mine is death. Prove it to yourself.

Torquemada was no coward; he knew that he had to see if the thing was speaking the truth, but he would not touch the man's blood himself and he could not have Francisco do it. What other choices did he have? His eyes lit on the back of the jailer, who, feeling them, turned in terror as he read the passing thought in Torquemada's mind. He fell to his knees, begging him not to do it. In the name of Jesus, he pleaded not to have to touch the demon or his blood. Torquemada felt a little guilty at the thought, which he dismissed a bit regretfully, but there had to be another way. The scurrying of a rat broke into his thoughts. That was the answer.

He ordered the jailer, "Bring me one of those! That will be how we shall test his threats."

Eagerly, the jailer ran off to do his bidding. He knew that the rats were nearly as tame as cats, for here they were always well fed and none were able to hurt them. It didn't take long before he returned with a sack that wriggled and jumped.

"I have found you a good one, Father. He is fat and healthy, and he nearly bit my nose off."

Torquemada couldn't bring himself to touch the filthy animal, and so he ordered the jailer to take the thing and put its mouth on the man's chest where the blood had clotted.

He did as he was commanded. Putting his hand into the sack, he cursed as the rat bit at him. He caught his finger before he managed to grasp the disgusting animal firmly by the back of its neck and withdraw it from the sack. It weighed nearly a pound and was black and gray, with red eyes that flashed hate at the thing holding him. It twisted and squirmed, trying to sink its teeth into any piece of flesh it could reach. The jailer pushed the animal's face to the chest of Casca. Without taking time to sniff its new target, the rodent sank its front incisors right into a patch of already dried and clotted blood and into the flesh of the man's chest.

Torquemada motioned to the jailer, and the rat was withdrawn. Even before they held it to the light, the rat went into spasms, its bowels opening, letting loose excrement. Its mouth opened spastically, its jaws snapping. Tiny legs vibrating, its body gave one great jerk, and then it died.

All three men went into a frenzy of crossing themselves and overlapping Hail Marys.

Shaking, Torquemada attempted to regain control of himself. "I believe you, demon. You will not be burned at the stake; neither shall your blood be spilled. But I cannot let you loose upon the world. Your case will have to be referred to the Holy Father in Rome. Until that time, you will remain here. "No one, save this man," he said, indicating the frightened jailer, "who has already witnessed your evil, will be permitted to see or speak to you on pain of death and certain excommunication. Those who disobey me shall never see their souls in heaven.

"You will not leave this cell until I have been instructed as to the best manner of disposing of you, and I assure you that the power of the Church will find a way."

CHAPTER TWO

As the cell door slammed, leaving him alone, Casca thought for a moment that he might have overdone it. He had saved himself a repeat bout with the thumbscrew and probably the rack, but he was still chained and locked up. He was a little surprised when the food slot on his door opened the next day and he was fed. He had to promise the jailer that he wouldn't hurt him or cast any evil spells so that the man would give him some slack in his chains, allowing him at least to eat and stand to exercise a bit. That was a start. Food and water had been his greatest concern; at least they weren't going to try to starve him to death. This wasn't the first time he had been locked up in a dungeon and probably wouldn't be the last.

Carefully, he examined every stone and crevice, testing the mortar and seams, feeling beneath the layers of rotting straw under which crawled beetles and other vermin by the thousands. One time those beetles had been his only source of nourishment for over two years.

He could find no weak spots in the stone; therefore, it had to be the chains. The iron was not of the best quality, although the links were large and well forged. If he had time, he could get through them. After thinning out his options, he kept going back to the pile of crystalline urine in the corner of his cell. In the other cells, the chains would be oiled occasionally to keep them from rusting. If he could keep them from doing that to his, there might be a way to speed the process. If he could just get one of his arms free, he had no doubt about being able to get the other loose.

Whenever he used his bladder, it was on the chains. When he was still or sleeping, he set the links in the pile of crystallized uric acid he had moved over from the corner. Each day the chains rusted a millimeter more, and each time he would rub the tiny flakes away against the stones of the cell wall.

It was several weeks before Torquemada received a reply from Rome. In essence, it told him to handle things as he saw fit. The Holy Father had more important things on his mind than the disposition of a single possessed soul. Torquemada was troubled by the memory of what he had witnessed in the demon's cell. It haunted his dreams. He was afraid to sentence the thing to the auto-da-fé or spill its blood. (He didn't like to refer to the prisoner in human terms.) At last he decided that it could do no harm as long as it was locked up. That was the answer: Keep it locked up forever if need be or until it died of whatever natural cause presented itself.

In order to protect the world a bit further, he performed a high mass at the door of the cell, sprinkling the outside with holy water and placing a small silver cross, one blessed by the Pope himself, permanently on the door. Perhaps that would help to keep the evil contained. To do much more was too tiring; it drained him of energy, and he knew that he was growing weaker with each passing day. There was yet much to do to cleanse the world of heretics.

The months passed into years. Casca didn't know that during his confinement Columbus had gone to the New World and returned. After this, it didn't take the Spaniards long to begin establishing colonies in the New World, seeking fresh lands to exploit. All this took place in only a few short years after Columbus's return.

Torquemada died quietly in his sleep, only slightly troubled by the thought that he had left something undone. Father Francisco preceded him by two years, dying of dysentery. The chief jailer had become the guest of his own prison. Torquemada had not wanted him spreading stories about their strange guest; it would have upset the people. He used the well-known fact that the jailer had sexually abused several of the female prisoners as his reason for ordering the man's arrest. The jailer had beaten his brains out against the walls of his cell rather than face the same kind of treatment he had given to others for the last ten years.

The prisoner in the dungeons of Sevilla was now no more than another of the thousands who languished in cells, forgotten by the outside world, whose jailers didn't even know the reason they were being held, assuming only that their superiors knew what was right and would decide who should be set free. They did as they always had; they followed orders and fed and watered their guest without ever knowing the reason why he was there. Nor did they care.

It took Casca eighteen months to work through the first thick link of his chains and another three for the other, but at last he had his hands free. Now he had to wait and be patient. Sooner or later an opportunity would present itself and he would have a chance to get away.

Casca did not know it would be many years before such an opportunity would arise. But, then again, he had all the time in the world. Using his freedom of movement, he did his best to keep some muscle tone, exercising as much as his strength permitted, always waiting for the door to open. He heard the jailers outside his door speak of Torquemada's death and wondered if that was why nothing more had been done to him.

For days he would lie by his door listening, trying to catch any word spoken between the guards that could give him information. Nothing! They came only at regular intervals to bring food and water, opening the small grill to insert his bowl after looking in to see whether he was where he was supposed to be. After they closed the grill, he could move to take his food. If he wasn't up against the wall, he wasn't fed. But they never entered the cell. All exchanges were made through the small grill.

Several times he attempted to trick the guards by groaning, howling, and scratching against the door. He even cried out that he was ready to tell them everything. But the door never opened, and the years went by. His skin turned the color of a fish's belly beneath his coating of grime and filth, and, even as it had at Helsfjord, his hair and beard grew into tangled

masses that served as home for a collection of insects and vermin.

Desperation forced his mind into fantastic schemes of
escape, and sadly he damned the name of He who had placed
the curse of life upon him. He had greater fears by far than
death and had met most of them in his centuries. Time and
again he had tried to die, and always the words of Jesus
mocked him at the crucial moment when he pleaded for death:

*Soldier, you are content with what you are, and that you
shall remain until we meet again.*

So were the words of Jesus by which he condemned Casca
to walk the earth until the Second Coming, a coming for
which Casca prayed most earnestly, one that would bring an
end to his wandering. To rest in the long sleep of eternity was
his greatest wish. But he lived. Although swords and spears
had struck blows that should have killed, death was denied
him. Even when he tried to commit suicide, it was to no avail;
he was condemned to live. *Suicide.* The thought kept returning, taking form slowly. Perhaps that was his way out. If he
was dead, they would have to take the body. It didn't take
long for him to come to a decision once he accepted the idea.

The next morning, when the jailers opened the grill, instead
of seeing the prisoner seated with his back against the wall,
they saw him hanging, his chains wrapped around his neck,
the thick links cutting deeply into the flesh of his throat. His
feet reached to the ground, but the legs were bent. It was his
own body weight that had done the deed. They watched for a
couple of minutes. Seeing no sign of life, they called for slaves
to come and remove the corpse.

Two Moriscos, kept by the prison for such a purpose, unwrapped the thick links from around the neck under the
scrutiny of one of the guards, who noted the swollen and
discolored face, the purple lips, and the twisted angle of the
prisoner's head. He was most definitely dead. The Moriscos,
looking more like beggars from the streets of Baghdad than
the rich merchants they once had been, grunted under the load
of their cargo, though by now Casca weighed a third less than
when he'd been brought to the dungeons. Dragging him by the
heels, they pulled him from his cell to the two-wheeled carrion
cart.

Escorted by the guard, the slaves rolled their load down

over the stones of the dungeon hallway to a barred door
leading to the outside world. If Casca's eyes had been able to
see the brightness of the early morning, they would have been
blinded for some time. The Moriscos talked softly in a mixture
of Spanish and Arabic till the escort gave them a look that
silenced their lips for the rest of the trip. They headed for a
place outside the city walls that was reserved for dungeon
guests who had expired.

Casca wasn't the only one to be tossed into the pit recently.
He didn't feel the shovels of earth covering his face and body.
Beneath him lay the decaying remains of others who had made
the trip from their cells to this spot. The dirt was shoveled
loosely over the victims, leaving room for those who would
surely come, if not tomorrow, then the next day. Rather than
digging separate graves each day, it saved time and ground
space to dig just one large pit and fill it with layers of bodies.
There was only enough soil shoveled in to keep the worst of
the stench from seeping out.

Townsmen and travelers avoided the graveyard of the
dungeon as if it bore the plague. Perhaps they felt that the
odds of their becoming residents also made it uncomfortable
to be very close to it.

Casca couldn't know that on this same day, October 6,
1516, a man in the colony at the island of Cuba was planning a
great adventure, one that would return him to his distant past.

As he lay in his grave, clouds began to gather. Racing in
from the sea, riding the winds, they rose and fell and fought to
pull together, but they were always burned away by the sun.
They tried once more in the afternoon, this time staying a bit
longer before the sun seared them away with easy contempt.
Near Zaragosa, the clouds managed to let loose some rain, but
it never reached the earth. The heat of the ground and air
burned it off, sending it back up into the heavens to be blown
away and reabsorbed. Once more, when darkness came, the
clouds gathered their forces and attempted another assault.
Far out to sea they rallied their numbers, throwing their
masses together, joining with companies and battalions of
lesser clouds into a heaving dark horde that rode high and fast
in great circles above the earth. They waited for the winds;
then, when the time was right, they charged again over the
oceans, their armies sweeping onto the coasts of Spain. Dark

and rumbling, they rode rivers of wind, beating back the heat of the air left behind by the sun. They would win their battle this night and let loose the rains to soothe the burned plains and wash the streets of Sevilla clean for a time.

Under the loosely packed earth he waited, his neck twisted at an odd angle, his mouth filled with dirt. The first fat drops of rain fell, patting the earth singly and then in groups as the clouds joined their strength together and crashed into one another, creating waves of thunder to roll over the plains. Lightning broke the night into splintered fragments of eye-piercing brightness that shattered trees and burst stones where it struck.

The rain began to gather in pools, seeking the lowest point. Several broke out to run together, forming small streams flowing into gutters and ditches. One of these found its way into the burial pit. The loose earth thirstily sucked up the first attempt of the rain to fill the pit, but at last the earth was sated and could hold no more. The water went deep down into the loose soil, saturating it. With nowhere else to go, it began to fill the pit slowly.

The rain turned the dirt on Casca's body into a slimy quagmire. The moisture eased through the grains of earth into his mouth and over his eyes, bringing a coolness with it. Dissolving the loose earth, the rain washed away the foot of dirt over him, exposing his face to the storm. Lightning crashed again from the heavens, a bolt landing near the pit, the smell of ozone conflicting with that of decay.

The life-giving waters soaked into his exposed pores. The rain gathered in intensity and pounded at his body, each drop a tiny hammer that vibrated against his chest. He began to rise, limbs floating limp and loose as the water rose in the pit.

Others rose with him. Those who had been buried before him also began to rise and float. The pit became an obscene thing where rotting corpses bobbed and moved and individual limbs rose and fell on their own. Decaying heads of men and women appeared, teeth exposed in perpetual leers, some with eyes, some without, others with no arms where they had rotted or been eaten off.

Muddy water seeped down between the muscles of his throat, reaching into his stomach. As the rain beat at him, a hand twitched, the fingers opening slightly and then closing.

Tremors began to run along his legs as his chest heaved, forcing his lungs to expand and then contract, sucking in air. He
was coming back to life one more time.

A merchant from Segovia and his two Moorish slaves were
trying to find their way to the shelter of an inn near the walls
of Sevilla. Because of the dark and the blinding rain, they had
missed their turn. They came instead to the brink of the pit.
The merchant slipped, falling into the dark, rain-frothed
water. When one of his slaves extended an arm to aid his
master, he pulled out instead the corpse of a woman whose
hand came loose at the wrist, leaving the claw in the terrified
hand of the Moor, who got a good look at what he was
holding during a burst of lightning. In spite of knowing that it
meant death if he was heard, he cried out, "Allah!" Then he
and his companion turned, fleeing from this place of djinns
and demons, leaving their master and his mules to the care of
the succubi who swam in the muddy waters.

If they had stayed to see what occurred next, they both
might have died of heart attacks, as their master did when he
attempted to pull himself from the pool and found that he was
being held on to by the hand of a cadaver. He managed to
drag himself out, but the damnable thing wouldn't let go of
his leg. It kept clawing at him, and it was gaining strength. The
merchant screamed, but no one could have heard him over the
din of the storm. Even if they had, no one would have ventured out to see if he could help. This was not a time when men
went readily to another's aid.

The merchant grasped the exposed root of a tree to hold on
to, all the time crying out for mercy as the thing holding onto
his leg began to crawl slowly up his body, pulling itself on top
of him until he could feel the full weight of it on his back. The
smell of decay that came from the creature was overpowering.
The merchant screamed once more, but suddenly he felt a
crushing pain in his chest and knew that he was going to die.
Making one feeble attempt to cross himself before expiring, he
let go of the tree roots and slid back into the pit.

Casca rolled off the merchant's back when he'd let go of the
root. He slid off onto slimy ground as the merchant took his
place in the pit. Through sticky, pus-filled eyes, he looked at
the merchant's face in the water. The mouth was open as it
sank under the fluid. No bubbles came from the lungs, and so

Casca knew that there was nothing he could do for the man; he was already dead.

His head was still at the same odd angle it had assumed when they buried him. He rose to unsteady feet, knowing that he had to get some distance between him and Sevilla. This time fortune was with him. The merchant's mules had sought shelter near the walls of the city. It didn't take him long to find the ropes and drag them, with stumbling steps, away from Sevilla. He would inspect the contents of the packs later.

Once in the clear, Casca took time to go through the merchant's belongings. Inside, he found clothes that were good enough for him to pass for a reasonably successful looking caballero, along with many items for trade. Most of the packs held samples of wares from Africa, France, and Italy—mostly bales of brightly colored cloth and a few fine yards of polychrome silks. In another pack he found foodstuffs carried for the merchant's journey. These he especially appreciated, as he did the use of the man's razor and soap at a stream when the storm passed. A bit of scraping, rubbing, and cursing, and Casca looked surprisingly fit.

He kept away from Sevilla and took the road to Cartagena. This took three days, during which time his neck returned nearly to normal. For a time he was afraid that it would never straighten out.

At Cartagena, it took but a few hours for him to trade his goods in for enough money to buy a sword of fair steel, one that had seen good service. It left him enough castellanos to provide for his needs for several months if he was frugal and if he abstained from wine and whores.

Taking quarters at an inn, he promised himself to keep away from wine. As for women, he knew that might be a bit tougher after his long confinement. In fact, it was impossible. Before he spent all his money on the wenches, the talk in the inn and city about the New World kept him from going broke.

He liked the idea of moving on and leaving Spain and the Inquisition behind. The New World offered riches, land, and slaves for the taking. He had heard promises like those many times before; they didn't interest him, but the talk of the New World did. Drawing what information he could out of some sailors, he gained a general idea of the location of the Spanish acquisitions and the placement of the island of Cuba. From there he knew that the Spanish would, if they hadn't already, come across the lands of the Teotec and other nations, peopled by fierce, intelligent natives who built temples and cities to their gods that rivaled those of ancient Rome and even Egypt.

Even with Torquemada dead, the Inquisition was still in force in Spain and most of Catholic Europe. He had no desire to share in its blessings any further. Perhaps in Cuba he might be able to lose himself and walk once more the great lane leading to the Pyramid of the Serpent in the city of Teotihuacan. He had lost much there. Maybe if he returned, he could find some of that which was taken from him over a thousand years ago. A thousand years? He was beginning to think that Jesus would never return. Several times over the centuries, he had gone to see those who were thought or proclaimed to be the returning Messiah. But all were fakes, although he had liked the old reprobate Mohammed quite a bit.

His next task wasn't too difficult. There was a steady stream of ships leaving Spain for Cuba and the New World. Using most of his money, he made purchases of a used breastplate, a helmet in the Spanish style, and most important, a horse trained for war. If there was employment for him in the New World, having his own horse would give him an advantage. His last purchase was a one-way ticket on a caravel bound for Cuba.

CHAPTER THREE

From the roof garden of his palace in the great city of Tenochtitlán, the king-god Moctezuma set aside his robe of rare feathers and removed from his wrists and arms the bands of beaten gold that were set with emeralds. Stroking the thin hairs of his mustache, he watched the sun set, casting pathways of shimmering gold streaming over the dark waters of the sacred lake Texcoco. Torches set in gold brackets cast a red glow over his sun-dark features. His face was troubled; worry lines creased the high, noble brow.

There had been portents and signs that disaster would soon walk the lands of the Aztecs. For the last five years, there had been increasing signs from the gods that they were not pleased with their children, the sons of Itzcoatl, the great king who had led the Aztecs to greatness, and Tlacealel, who had proved their descent from the god of war, Huitzilopochtli, and had given them their laws, always ensuring that the sun would not die by offering to him a constant stream of human sacrifices to feed on.

The first omen had appeared in the eastern sky—a flaming ear of corn. It bled fire drop by drop, as if the heavens themselves were wounded. Wide at the base and narrowing at the peak, it burned in the very heart of heaven, only to fade with the coming of the sun, then to reappear each night for a full year, beginning in the year 12 House. The people were frightened and in wonder of the meaning of the omen. When the skies themselves bled, it could bode only ill for mere mortals.

The second sign came when the temple of Huitzilopochtli burst spontaneously into flames on the site of Tlacateccan (the house of authority). And there had been others: lightning appearing on a clear day to strike sacred places and fire racing through the skies in broad daylight in three streams to where the sun rises, the tails giving off showers of sparks to burn and fade like the coals of an oven. Even increasing the sacrifices threefold had not brought any change in the signs.

Moctezuma moved closer to his balcony, where the breeze from the lake cooled the evening air. From this height, he could see the lake and the torches on the prows of distant fishing boats where the fishermen were gathering their harvest for the marketplaces on the morrow. His slaves had been dismissed to return to their barracks, leaving him alone with the heavens. Only his guards, knights from the Clan of the Eagle, armed with the *macama*, a wooden club lined with chips of obsidian or flint, so sharp that a man could shave with one, stood near his doors with orders to permit no one to disturb his thoughts this night.

Why had his dreams been so tortured? Was he not greatly loved by his people? So much so that on the day of his ascendance to power, they had honored him by sending the still-beating hearts of twenty-five thousand messengers to the gods as a token of their love.

To the south, he could see the fires of the priests burning brightly on their altars at the great pyramid of the Teocalli. On his orders, they were sending the red flowers to the gods in an unending stream, imploring them to accept the offering of burned hearts and end the nightmare dreams that plagued their master.

To the northeast, heat lightning rippled over the ancient city of the gods, Teotihuacan. It had been there centuries before the Aztecs had made their migrations from the north out of the deserts. They had found a few inhabitants remaining who had told them of the city and their chief deity, the Quetzalcoatl, whose symbol was the Feathered Serpent. From those few remnants of the once great Teotec and the Toltecs, they had acquired the worship of the Quetza, fitting him into their pantheon. The god was not of the same bloody mind as their own deities, but if he could found such a city as this and be worshiped by tribes reaching beyond those of the Maya to the south, then he must be powerful and not be offended.

In one of the temples of the old city, the savage Aztecs had found masks of jade still cared for by the one remaining priest of the city. Disease had taken all the others long ago. From him they had learned of how the Quetza, a light-haired, fair-skinned god, and his shining warriors had come from the sea riding on a Feathered Serpent and brought peace to the city after defeating the armies of the Olmec king, Teypeytal.

Of late, Moctezuma had visited the city and its shrine where the masks were cared for by their new priests, those of his race. Often he had looked upon the face of the god from the sea, the eyes of blue-gray set in the jade mask, the scar running from one eye to the corner of the mouth. It was a face unlike any of his race or those of the smoking lands. According to the priest of Teotihuacan, the Quetza had promised to return one day. The *tlamatinime* (wise men) had read the signs and given that date as 1 Reed, which occurred every fifty-two years. 1 Reed would come again in five years.

Perhaps that was what the omens from the heavens were trying to tell him. The Feathered Serpent was going to return, and he would not be pleased at the changes that had taken place. For he was a strange god who demanded no human sacrifice. Indeed, according to the last priest, his teachings forbade it. This was not logical, and those who had spoken to the last priest of the Teotec said that he was nearly mad and that many of his words made no sense. Therefore, they honored the Quetza as they did their own, with sacrifices.

The Aztec kings and nobles believed, as did the wise men, that for their race there was only one great god, Huitzilopochtli. All the others were only his different aspects, both male and female, by which means it was easier for the peasants and slaves to understand the awesome power of the creator. Could it be that the Feathered Serpent was another of those faces? But he had not been born of their people. The legend of the Quetza had been old before the first of the Aztecs had entered the valley. Perhaps he was an older and wiser god than

Huitzilopochtli? Moctezuma mentally chastised himself for his doubts as to the power of the giver and taker of life, the living sun.

Still it was said that disaster would come if the people of the valley spilled human blood in sacrifice. Many of the original inhabitants of Teotihuacan had reverted to their old practices of human sacrifice, and a series of droughts and plagues had nearly wiped them out. Was it the Serpent punishing them for disobeying his commandments? And if so, would he punish the Aztecs because they were now the people of the valley? Moctezuma was terribly confused, for he was a pious man and an initiate of the priesthood. He could not deny his gods their due, for that was to invite disaster, too. Yet if the Serpent did return, how should he be greeted? Could a mortal man go against the will of a god? Would Huitzilopochtli help him against the Serpent?

Moctezuma decided that he had to do more to make certain he would gain the favor of the giver and taker of life. In the morning he would order his warriors to go forth and return with no fewer than twenty thousand captives for the altars. That should give him some peace of mind for a time.

CHAPTER FOUR

The long journey to the New World began auspiciously enough, with fair winds pushing at the two masts of the caravel. The ship had the smell common to all sailing vessels: wet tar and hemp from the lines and the sour odor of sunburned bodies performing the thousand tasks necessary to keep the ship from rotting away.

Captain Jaime Ortiz was a master of the old school, believing in the lash or a knot of the ship's rope to enforce discipline as his ship's priest read from the Bible. Ortiz was a most Catholic man who saw evil in everything that was not understood. Stern, hawk-nosed, spade-bearded, and dark as a Moor from his years under the sun, he stood on the upper deck dressed in total black, with a sterile white neck ruff as his single ornament. His eyes never resting, he missed nothing in the skies or on board his vessel. As he stood by the wheel, hand to his sword, he ruled over those beneath him as if he had God's mandate.

Casca tried his best to keep his distance from the captain. He had seen too many men with that same sternness of spirit that allowed no compassion for anyone who was not of their faith or nation. It was a certainty that if he and the captain ever exchanged more than a few words, it would lead to trouble, which he could ill afford. He'd had enough of the good Christians of Spain. That was one of his main reasons for taking the ship to the New World, the farther the better. His recent experiences with the Grand Inquisition of the Dominican priest, Torquemada, and his relish for the auto-da-fé proved that Spain was no place for one such as he.

Among the other passengers, there was to be found the usual mixture of priests out to gain new souls for Mother Church: indentured men and women, gentlemen adventurers seeking their fortunes, men on the run from the law, and the scavengers who went to feed on what their betters would leave behind. Of those on board the rolling, ungainly vessel, there were some who paid for their passage with their sweat. These had it worse than the regular seamen, for they were neither part of the crew nor counted among the passengers, and the good captain, Señor Ortiz, knew the value of them as compared to his regular crew. Therefore, they were given the most dangerous jobs, as they were more expendable and their death or injury would be less of a loss to the ship than those of his regular crew. It was one of these semislaves who brought Casca into his first confrontation with Ortiz.

Four days out, the first heavy swells began to push at the stern as the winds began. At first, only a light froth whipped the tops of the waves as the swells gradually became deeper and longer. The caravel rode up and then slid down them under the force of the gathering storm. On the sixth day, the winds from the north hit in their full fury, driving the ungainly vessel deeper into the swells until the mainsails had to be lowered. Only the top gallants were kept aloft to give the ship some control over her forward momentum. If the mainsails had been left up, the force of the wind would have driven the ship bow first into the watery valleys to be swallowed up and never seen again.

With the winds came the clouds, black thunderheads of cracking violence that turned day into near night. Captain Ortiz stayed at his post for the first two days, eating by the wheel and shouting commands through his horn. He played his ship in the storm as a musician does his instrument, riding the tempo of the waves, gauging every movement and pause, and taking advantage of any weakness in the winds to better his position. Hanging on for life, the able-bodied seamen went into the upper rigging to reef sails and tighten lines. Cargo was lashed down in the holds, and the horses were blindfolded to keep them in place in the event of panic. Casca stayed on the upper decks, not wanting to be below if the ship was driven under.

The main sails were being ripped into shreds and had to be retied to keep them from being torn completely away. A cry from aloft was barely audible over the scream of the wind through the humming lines. The seaman's body was ripped from the rigging to fly with the winds, bouncing off the center mast, until his spine cracked. The body was blown away with a sheet of torn sail to be lost in the froth-driven waters of the Atlantic. Ortiz screamed for another man to take his place in the swaying, rain-lashed heights above the ship.

"You, *hombre!*" He pointed his horn at the lower deck. "Get aloft and help secure those sails!"

Holding on to a stanchion, a diminutive figure tried to keep from being thrown over the side. It was to him that Ortiz had made his command. Juan de Castro turned his eyes to the swaying, dizzying heights of the storm-lashed upper mast. His stomach started to turn in on itself at the thought of climbing up those thin, wet, slippery lines. The winds were beginning to shift, trying to turn the caravel sideways where the deep, green-black waters could wash over her sides. Ortiz lashed at the helmsman, straining against the wheel with two ordinary seamen helping to control the rudder under his direction. The ship slipped sideways and rolled as de Castro grasped wet lines to begin hauling his thin body up into the rigging. He was barely able to get his feet on the ropes and hold on, much less climb. A hand grasped his leg, jerking him back to the deck. Its eyes nearly blinded by the beating rains, a square face looked down at him.

"Stay here. If you go up, you'll just get yourself killed and someone else will have to go anyway."

De Castro would have protested, but the man already was clambering up into the lines. With practiced hands and feet, the climber balanced himself against the movement of the ship. Ortiz watched the exchange but couldn't move to do anything about it. The man, now high in the yards, was not one of those who were working their way across. He was a paying passenger and had no right to interfere with his lawful orders as commander of this vessel. If the smaller man had died, it would have mattered little, for that was part of his bargain. If one signed on as a seaman, it was not unreasonable to expect that person to perform the duties of one, no matter what the risk, for that was in the hands of God.

Hanging on to the spars, Casca had a vision of being blown off the rigging to be lost in the heaving seas beneath him. He cursed himself for being a fool and giving in to a whim of the moment. Beside him, in the same condition, were others of the crew, their feet resting on swaying lines beneath the spars. They bent over and hauled the heavy, wet sails back up to tie them down again. Fingers bled from the wet lines as flesh peeled off the palms of hands and fingers. Faces blinded by the winds and rain, they worked for over an hour to get the last of the sails properly secured. Only then could they come down. If they failed to perform their task, it would not be a much worse fate to let the winds and seas have them rather than face the wrath of the ship's master and his lash.

Taking his time, arms and legs trembling from the strain, Casca began the climb back down to the deck. No sooner had his feet touched down than the second mate yelled for him to go to his quarters and remain there until the captain sent for him. He received several pitying glances from the crewmen who had been aloft with him. De Castro went with Casca to where he shared his quarters with three others in the cramped space of the lower foredeck.

Once inside and out of the rain, all they had to contend with was the heaving of the ship itself. Rummaging through his bag, Casca found a semidry shirt that was only a bit green from mold. Drying his upper body as best he could with it, he ignored de Castro's look of wonder at the scars on his torso. He was used to the effect his body had on others. They sat side by side on his bunk, feet resting against the other side to stabilize them. Casca waited for whatever it was de Castro was going to say. Clearing his throat, the smaller man tried to put his words in order. He was a man of good though poor family and, like most of those born to Castile, had an overdeveloped sense of pride.

"Señor . . . ?" He paused, not knowing Casca's name.

Adjusting his body to where it rested more securely against

the ship's planking, Casca told him, "Romano, Carlos Romano."

De Castro tried once more: "Señor Romano, I wish to thank you for your noble gesture, but I assure you, I was quite capable of performing the task myself."

Casca smiled at him. "That's bullshit, and you know it. Look at your hands. Those wet lines would have ripped them apart, and from the color of your face, you don't handle rough seas very well to begin with. Let us just say I performed a service for a gentleman, and one day you may have the opportunity to return the favor."

De Castro accepted the terms; at least it returned some of his pride to him. "That is a duty I shall consider an honor from one caballero to another. Will you take the hand of Juan de Castro on it as a pledge of my friendship?"

Casca looked the smaller man over. Although the face was thin and drawn, with no more than twenty-five or twenty-six years in it, there was a sincerity to it that touched him. De Castro was obviously one who had come upon bad times and was going to the New World to rebuild his life. While his body was not that of a strong man, there was a litheness to it, and the wrists had strong bands of tendons that showed that this was one who had spent his youth mastering the sword.

Casca took Juan's hand. "I accept your offer gladly and return your pledge with my own. In these new lands, who can know when it will be good to have one at your side or back you can trust?"

With those words the men made a bond to be compadres, sharing whatever came against them.

Captain Ortiz had no such feelings for the two men. He was master of his ship, and every word he spoke was the law. There was no other way to control such animals as he had in his crew. They respected only power and fear. Absolute obedience was the only true law of the sea. The wind shifted again, and he called out new orders to compensate for it. From the taste of the wind, he knew that they had reached the peak of the storm. From here on out, it would diminish; then he would see to the men below.

By sunfall the following day, the storm had passed over, leaving the seas glassy smooth and calm, with just enough wind to fill the sails gently. Ortiz went to his cabin. He would see to his problems in the morning, after he had slept. He turned control of the caravel over to his second mate, Luis Vargas, a man who had risen to his current position primarily because of his ability to get the most out of his crew. When Vargas swung the lash or knotted piece of ship's rope, it left a lasting impression on both the body and the soul of the man who experienced it. Short in size, he was nearly as wide at the shoulders as he was tall, and he could perform any task on the ship faster and better than any of the crew. He drove those in his charge to meet his standards, which they never did. He and his captain made a perfect team. Ortiz, with his fine manners and disdain for those beneath him, gave Vargas all the opportunities he needed to enforce his own manner of discipline on the crew, a task Vargas took great pride in. Never in his twenty-two years at sea had there been a man under him whom he could not beat at any game of strength.

Shortly after dawn, Casca and Juan were sent for. Luis Vargas escorted them personally to the captain's cabin. Knocking on the door with calloused knuckles, Vargas was given permission to enter. He let the two men enter first and then followed after them, closing the door behind him. The captain's cabin was much the same as the captain himself. It was spare in creature comforts; the only furniture was a single narrow bunk and a desk with two chairs in front of it. The rest of the cabin was lined with racks for his charts and ship's papers. Near his bed was a small altar on which an image of the Blessed Virgin waited patiently for his prayers.

As always, Captain Ortiz was dressed in a black suit with a single white ruff around his neck. He motioned for Casca to take one of the two chairs. When Juan started to take the other, he was brought up short by a jerking motion of the captain's hand and a terse reminder: "Señor de Castro, you are not a paying passenger; therefore, you will remain standing." Casca saw the flush of embarrassment rush to Juan's face, but Juan did as he was ordered, for the captain was correct. Ortiz turned his attention to Casca. "As for you. You, señor, are a passenger. That entitles you to certain privileges aboard my ship, but it does not permit you to interfere with my lawful commands to a member of my crew."

Juan started to protest, extending his right hand out to draw the captain's attention. This was halted by the thick meaty fingers of Vargas grasping his wrist. An involuntary grunt of pain broke from Juan's lips as Vargas increased the pressure. Vargas was concentrating on the force he was applying and didn't notice Casca rising from his chair until his own wrist was trapped in the sinewy, knotted hand of the one-time galley slave. From Vargas there came an involuntary grunt of pain. Casca sent strength down his arms to his fingers, forcing Vargas's hand open until he released Juan's wrist.

Vargas tried to twist out of the grip only to find that he was being forced to his knees; tears welled up in his eyes. He could feel the bones in his wrist starting to rub together. If the pressure increased, the bones would snap like green twigs.

Ortiz rose from his chair only to sit back down once more when Casca pointed his free hand at him, speaking very quietly and gently: "I believe that our problem stems from Juan de Castro not being a paying passenger. Am I correct?"

Ortiz nodded his head in affirmation. Casca gave Vargas's wrist a bit more of a squeeze, forcing another groan from the man.

"Then, Señor Captain, I propose that we put this unpleasantness behind us by your permitting me to lend Señor de Castro enough money to pay for his passage from the day we left port in Spain. By doing this, Señor de Castro would have to be considered as a full fare from that time and there could be no hint of disrespect to you or your command."

One of Vargas's wrist bones began to crack. The pain was so great, he couldn't even strike at the hand holding him. Captain Ortiz made up his mind quickly. After all, money was worth more than another nearly useless mouth to feed. In addition, the logic of the argument was irrefutable. It would save his pride, and he was certain that no word of what had happened in this cabin would be bandied about.

"Señor Romano, I accept your offer—trusting, of course, in your discretion concerning this matter."

Casca agreed and released Vargas, who rolled away quickly to rest on his haunches, holding his nearly broken limb with his good hand. From the look in Vargas's eyes, Casca knew that there probably would be trouble yet to come. To try to avoid this, before leaving the cabin, he gave a veiled warning to Ortiz.

"There is yet a long way to go before we reach Cuba, Captain. I would hate to have our journey interrupted by any further unpleasantness. For if that did happen, I would feel compelled to address the matter to you personally—in the strongest manner I am capable of."

Ortiz knew exactly what the scar-faced man meant. He nodded his understanding as the door closed behind them.

Vargas made no overt move against Casca and Juan, but he never stopped watching them or remembering the humiliation of the way he had been treated in front of his captain. Ortiz had not said anything to him; he merely looked at him with contempt and dismissed him as he would a common deck-hand. As the days passed, the fair winds did nothing to decrease the growing hatred he felt for the two men. In time he had found a dozen reasons for his not being able to break the steel grasp of the one called Romano. His treatment of his crew became even harsher as he fought to regain his self-esteem by abusing those beneath him. And with each act of domination, his courage began to return. Hate combined with renewed confidence gave him all the more reason to take revenge. He knew that Captain Ortiz would not be displeased if the two somehow met with a fatal accident before they reached Havana. He would wait and mark time until the proper opportunity presented itself.

Casca and Juan spent their hours in swordplay, as did most of those who planned on winning their fortunes in the New World on the point of their weapons. Juan had a good wrist and used it to his advantage, often parrying Casca's strong thrusts with little effort. Casca didn't let him know that this was done with his help. He wanted to build the smaller man's confidence in himself. Subtly, he let Juan learn techniques that he had not been taught in the fencing schools of Spain, techniques that could well mean the difference between life and death for the young man. Only Casca had any idea of what they might have to face if things went as he thought they would and the Spanish at last found their way to the lands where dark-skinned warriors wore the bright, rainbow-colored feathers of rare birds and human sacrifices had been and might still be made on stone altars to terrible and bloody gods.

He liked the young man, though he knew that pride such as Juan felt had led to thousands of deaths in the past and would cause even more in the future. He knew better than to try to change the customs and teachings of generations overnight. But if Juan survived, time might be the best instructor of all. Juan's physical strength was not great, but he wasn't lacking in courage. He would do. If he lived long enough, he might even achieve that which he sought; namely, to rebuild his family's fortune and return to Spain in the manner befitting a grandee of Castile.

They reached the southern waters, where the sky and winds grew warmer and dolphins raced in front of the ship as if they were welcoming or guiding the caravel to a safe harbor. The waters became crystal clear, where a man could look down through the depths over thirty meters and see the animals of the warm seas as clearly as if they were in a fishbowl. Islands appeared with increasing frequency, green palm-dotted spots of land that beckoned them to stop and rest. But Ortiz had no mind for such things and made only one short detour to a flat, isolated island less than two miles around. This was done only to replenish their supply of fresh water, and no one other than the landing party was permitted to leave the ship. Once the kegs had been filled at a spring and brought back on board, they set sail for the last leg of their journey. Cuba was now only a three-day sail.

Luis Vargas had observed his quarry long enough to know their patterns. Juan and his ugly friend had made a habit of rising with the predawn to come on deck and take the morning air. It was their custom to sit on the railings by the bow and face into the path of the ship. It should not be too difficult to arrange an accident. He was not concerned about Casca; he knew that he could take care of him. If he waited in the shadows, two quick strikes with a belaying pin would take care of them, and both would be over the side in less time than a heartbeat. He'd take out the scarred one first and then the youngster. With surprise on his side, he had no doubt about his ability to accomplish his desire. Let them swim to Cuba.

The nights had become heavy and oppressive in the small confines of the tiny cabin. Casca had always been an early riser and used this as a chance to go to the upper decks, where the breeze from the sea could wipe away the cobwebs of a troubled sleep filled with night sweats. Juan had taken to accompanying him. It seemed as if the hours before the dawn were when the soul was most awake. They'd sit on the bow and talk of many things, some in the past and some yet to come. De Castro was amazed at how much history his new friend knew. Although much of what this man, Romano, said was near heresy or even treason, there was something in the voice that said he was telling the truth or at least the truth as he believed it.

Vargas stood by the sail locker, hidden in the shadows, waiting for his quarry to present itself. He enjoyed the anticipation of the coming event. He would redeem himself in the eyes of Captain Ortiz, and then all would be well. A head came up from the stairwell leading below deck. It was joined by another. Casca and Juan took their time walking with the roll of the ship toward the bow. Vargas sucked in his breath, holding it in as his heart began to beat faster. As the two men neared him, his hand gripped the belaying pin tighter. His muscles tensed, his legs beginning to tremble at the strain of containing his desire. He wanted Romano; the other was just an added bonus. Casca was in the lead. That was good. He'd brain him first and then smash the smaller man before he had time to react or cry out.

It would have gone as he planned if fate hadn't taken a hand. As Casca passed him, Vargas moved out to strike, his arm rising to crush the belaying pin down on the skull of his prey. Unfortunately for him, when he raised his arm up with the pin, he hit the side of the sail locker. Casca turned in time to catch the blow on his left forearm. The heavy hardwood pin nearly broke the bone. He turned under the blow, dropping his body and shoulder down at right angles to his attacker. Casca lowered his body to where his shoulder was on a level with Vargas's waist. Vargas's own momentum threw him onto Casca's shoulder. Grasping Vargas by the tunic with his free hand, Casca thrust back up with his leg muscles, raising Vargas off the deck, waist over his shoulder.

When his shoulder hit Vargas in the gut, it took the air out of the second mate. He was still trying to suck in a breath as Casca twisted and turned, heaving him into the air. The second mate just had time to take one quick breath before he hit the water. Juan never had time to do anything. The whole event was a blur. When all this was over, Casca had a feeling that the events were vaguely familiar, and he recalled a distant moment when he had performed much the same act while passing through the Straits of Messina.

The watch on the quarterdeck heard a cry for help come from the starboard side. He knew the voice well; it had chewed him out more than once and mocked him as it meted out twenty lashes with the knot. The seaman rushed to the side and looked down. He saw Casca and Juan standing there, looking back to where the voice now cried less loudly for help. The watch had a pretty good idea of what had taken place. He looked about to see whether anyone else had heard Vargas's cry. There was no sign of it. He returned to his watch rather pleased that he had been able to settle the score with the second mate at no risk to himself.

Juan knew that Vargas had been trying to kill them, and he considered the man no great loss. One who came from the shadows at night was most certainly a person without any sense of honor and therefore deserving of his watery fate.

In the morning, without having any witnesses to call on, Captain Ortiz had to enter into his log that the second mate, Luis Vargas, had been lost overboard some time during the night. He tried to read the expressions of Juan and Casca, who merely smiled and winked at him. Ortiz felt quite uneasy at that and was glad that they would be in the safe port of Havana in only two more days. Then he would be rid of his troublesome cargo. As for Vargas, there was something about the man he would miss, but there had never been a shortage of those with the same qualities. Vargas's position would not be very difficult to fill.

CHAPTER FIVE

In color and design, Havana was much like any town of Spain. Only the tropical winds from the warm seas gave the air a heavy feel that was not of Castile. Near the tavern of the Dos Dracos, two men pushed their way through the early evening crowd of soldiers, sailors, Indian slaves, and mestizo whores. They were going to the inn for a particular purpose. Hernan Cortes was outfitting an expedition to the New World. He was signing on men for that adventure now.

Casca Longinus, now called Carlos Romano, took his place in line at the doorway to the Dos Dracos, standing behind a sailor with bare feet and calloused broad hands suited for raising a sail or swinging a cutlass. Over the mass of heads, he could see the interior of the tavern. It was crowded with all that was the best and worst of Spain, men of great pride and quick tempers who prided themselves on their piety and fear of God as they did on their ability to lie and kill. Most of those signing the articles were much like him. They brought their own weapons and armor if they had it. There would be no pay, only a share of the loot if there was any. Casca was one of the few who had no real interest in the gold of the Indians nor in their silver and women. Neither did he have the burning desire to save their souls by bringing the cross to replace their heathen idols. His was another purpose, a reason that came from centuries before.

Juan stood behind his larger friend near the rear rank of the soldiers and sailors gathered to hear Cortes make his speech. The man had a way with words and men; Casca would give him that. But he had a premonition that Cortes was not one who would let much, if anything, stand in the way of his desires. Cortes removed his polished steel helmet as he began, his voice reaching easily over the heads of those assembled on the docks.

"Certain it is, my friends and companions, that every good man of spirit desires and strives by his own effort to make himself the equal of the excellent men of his day and even those of the past." At this, Casca barely controlled a derisive laugh, not that it would have stopped the words that followed. "And so it is that I am embarking upon a great and beautiful enterprise, one which will be famous in times to come, because I know in my heart that we shall take vast and rich lands, peoples such as have never before been seen, and kingdoms greater than those of our monarchs. Certain it is also that the lust for glory extends beyond this mortal life and that taking a whole world will hardly satisfy it, much less one or two kingdoms.

"I have assembled ships, arms, horses, and the other materials of war, a great stock of provisions, and everything else commonly needed and profitable in conquest. I have spent large sums, for which I have put in pawn my own estates and those of my friends. For it seems to me that the less I retain of it, the greater will be my honor. Small things must be given up when great things present themselves. I hope in God that more profit will come to our king and nation from our expedition than from those of all others. I need hardly mention how pleasing it will be to God, our Lord, for love of whom I have willingly offered my toil and my estate; nor shall I speak of the danger to life and honor to which I have exposed myself in getting the fleet together, because I would have you know that I do not seek gain from it so much as honor, for good men hold honor dearer than riches."

Casca thought that Cortes did very well in bringing up things he didn't want to mention. The man was a natural politician. Cortes caught his breath and continued.

"We are engaging in a just and good war which will bring us fame. Almighty God, in whose name and faith it will be waged, will give us victory, and time will see the accomplishment that always follows upon whatever is done and guided by intelligence and good counsel. We must, therefore, employ a different way, a different reasoning, and a different skill from those of Cordoba and Grijalba. I shall not pursue the matter further because of the pressure of time, which urges us onward. There we shall do as we shall see fit, and here I offer you great rewards, although they will be wrapped about with great hardships. Valor loves not idleness, and so therefore, if you will take hope for valor, or valor for hope, and if you do not abandon me, as I shall not abandon you, I shall make you in a very short time the richest of all men who have crossed the seas and of all the armies which have made war. You are few, I see, but such is your spirit that no effort or force of Indians will prevail against you, for we have seen by experience how God has favored the Spanish nation in these parts and how we have never lacked courage or strength and never shall. Go your way now, content and happy, and make the outcome equal to the beginning."

The assembly gave a great cheer, much encouraged by the speech, especially the part about making them rich men. There was a rush for the assembly to line up in three rows to sign the articles that would make them part of this great enterprise. Casca and Juan waited their turn, the scar-faced man thinking of the manner in which fate turns its endlessly spinning wheel of chance. If Grijalba and Cordoba had not made a chance landing on the shores of the unknown lands to the west of Cuba, Cortes would not at this time be signing on hands to go there.

Cortes waited until all had signed the articles and then stood on a table to get their attention once more. To all there, he gave the order that they were to sail as soon as a mass was said and the wind turned favorable. Men rushed to gather their gear and load equipment and horses. They would be ready when the time came.

It was February 18, 1519, when Cortes gave his pilots their orders and set a large lantern from his mast to serve as a guide for the others of his small fleet. The course was set for due west of Punta de San Anton, the last tip of Cuba, for Cape Catoche, the closest landfall at Yucatan, sixty leagues distant.

The conquistadors of Spain had set sail.

A storm blew up that night, and they were forced to change their course. Instead of Yucatan, they made first landfall on the island of Cozumel. Three ships of the fleet had managed to stay with Cortes's flagship, and of the rest, only one ship failed to find its way to Cozumel, though all of them were blown off course and had to pick their own paths and speed. The ship commanded by de Morala had lost its rudder in the storm, and this caused some delay before Cortes was able to press on.

Two more days' sail without sight of land and they reached Punta de las Mujeres, where they found several of the stray ships at anchor, waiting. Cortes ordered his pilots to set their course for the direction in which the winds and weather had most likely blown the remainder of his lost ships. He found them anchored in a fair harbor within sight of a native town. Ordering a patrol to investigate the village, Cortes hoped to find a friendly reception. But when they returned to the ships, it was with the word that all the natives had fled. When questioned further, they said that the town was well built of mortar and stone with roofs of thatch. They did return with some garments of cotton and a few pieces of gold jewelry found in the houses. There were several of what they believed to be temples and a high tower, but in those they found nothing. Outside the village there were fields of maize, orchards, and many beehives.

Cortes was pleased but also a bit surprised that the villagers had run away to hide in the woods. This was the same place where Juan de Grijalba had ventured to earlier. Fearing an ambush, he ordered fifty men and their horses to land, not only to search out the countryside but also to rest the animals and let them pasture. Casca was in the search party, being one of those who owned his own animal. He and ten others found five women and three children hiding in the brush. These they returned to Cortes, who naturally could not understand them. He managed by using signs, making them understand that he was not going to do them or their children any harm. One of the women was clearly the mistress of the others, and from the way the children clung to her, it was certain that she was also their mother. Casca watched with approval as Cortes put the weeping woman at her ease by giving her gifts of clothing, several small mirrors, and scissors, which astonished her when she understood their use. Once she no longer was in fear for her life, she requested permission to send one of her servants to speak to her lord and master to tell of the manner in which she had been treated.

It was several hours before six native men came to the town to see whether what the servant had said was true and whether the wife of the *calachuni* was actually being treated as an honored guest. They were given small gifts and sent back with the word that the Spaniards had come as friends and that the *calachuni* himself should come and see that he had no reason to fear them. The next morning the chief came, bringing gifts of honey, bread, and fish. This was the first opportunity Juan and Casca had to see Cortes in his element, that of winning the natives to his side. He was a natural diplomat. He ordered that all the things taken from the houses be brought to him, including the few items of gold and silver they had found. These he laid out so that their owners could identify and reclaim their possessions. These simple acts, so contrary to what Casca had seen of the normal Spanish method of dealing with what they considered to be inferior beings (and they considered everyone in the world inferior beings), left him sanguine. He had high hopes for his commander if Cortes conducted all of his business in the same manner.

Francisco de Cordoba, one of Cortes's captains, had in his company a man named Melchior, who had spent time as a fisherman in the coastal waters near Yucatan and had a small grasp of the tongue of the people of these regions. Although Melchior's abilities were limited, it was better than nothing. It was through him, accompanied by many signs and sand drawings, that Cortes was able to make most of his words known. The natives were impressed by the Spaniards, with their beards and fair skin, and especially by the horses, which they would watch for hours at a time. It was clear that they considered the Spaniards to be more than just ordinary men and therefore were not very upset when Cortes ordered their idols smashed and replaced with the cross. In this, Juan joined in with a fervor, for he was a good Catholic. Casca watched it all and wondered if all the natives they met would be as ready as these were to accept the new religion the Spaniards were offering them. Old ways die hard.

The Cacique, whose wife Cortes had treated so nobly, came to him after they had been there about ten days. He made signs to Cortes, pointing toward Yucatan, that he had heard of four or five other bearded men there. Upon considering how vital to his plans it would be to have someone who really could communicate with the natives, Cortes at last coaxed the Cacique into sending three men to the bearded men, even though they were afraid that if they were found out, they would be killed and eaten by the chieftain who held the bearded men captive. It took a few more bribes of trinkets before they were convinced to try. Cortes wrote a letter to the unknown captives, saying:

Noble lords,
   I have departed from Cuba with a fleet of eleven vessels and five hundred and fifty Spaniards and have arrived here at Cozumel, where I am writing this letter to you. The people of this island have assured me that in your country there are four or five bearded men like us in every respect. They cannot give me more details, but judging from what they have told us, I suspect and consider as certain that you are Spaniards. I and these gentlemen who have come with me to explore and colonize these lands beg you, within six days from the time you receive this letter, to come to us without delay or excuse. If you will come, we shall recognize and reward the favor that this fleet will receive from you. I am sending a brigantine to pick you up and two ships to act as escort.

Hernan Cortes
of Havana, Cuba

In order to keep the letter hidden, Cortes chose the brightest looking of the Indians and hid the letter in the man's thick braids. He sent Captain Escalante and his brigantine, along with Diego de Ordaz and several Indians, to command the two escort ships and the fifty soldiers on them. Escalante landed the Indians where he was told to, let them off, and waited seven days, though he had been told to wait for six. When the Indians didn't return, he figured they'd been found out and killed or taken as slaves. Cortes was disappointed that they had not returned with at least one Spaniard who could speak the tongue of the Indians. He gave the order for his fleet to make ready to sail.

The fleet had not cleared the cape before they had to put about and return to Cozumel, where Pedro de Alvarez's ship had sprung a leak so bad that not even two pumps could keep it under control. The Indians were glad to see them return, but Cortes was impatient, feeling that even nature and luck were beginning to conspire against his destiny. It was the following Sunday, which was the first day of Lent, when Cortes decided to hold a mass before they attempted to leave again. It was then that he was told that a canoe had been seen sailing from Yucatan to the island, heading for where his ships were anchored. Cortes put out a guard under the command of Andres de Tapia, the commander of his arquebusiers, in case the new arrivals were hostile. They went to the beach to await the arrival of whoever was coming from the mainland.

The log canoe touched the beach, and four men got out of it, all of them wearing only breechclouts, their hair braided over their foreheads, bows and arrows in their hands. Three of them started to try to get back into the boat when they saw the Spaniards of de Tapia coming at them with drawn swords. One stepped in front of them, speaking their tongue and halting their flight. Then he turned to those carrying the good steel of Toledo in their hands and cried out in Spanish, "Gentlemen, are you Christians?" When they affirmed that it was so, he broke into tears, sank to his knees, and begged them to do likewise. They joined him as he said thanks to God and the Holy Virgin for their mercy in restoring him to his country and out of the hands of the devils who had held him for so long.

Cortes was in a frenzy of delight over the man who identified himself as Gerónimo de Aquilar. Once the former captive had been cleaned up and clothed as befitted a Spanish gentleman, he was asked to accompany Cortes as his adviser and interpreter. He eagerly accepted. The story he told of his captivity left the caballeros of Cortes's company aghast at the barbaric habits of the natives of Yucatan. They vowed that they would teach civilized manners to any savages that they met, even if they had to burn them at the stake to do it.

Gerónimo, his face lean and darkened by years in the tropical sun, was full of expression as he related the tale of his being shipwrecked while on a mission with Vasco Nunez de Balboa for the admiral governor of Santo Domingo in the year 1511. He had been shipwrecked, losing not only his ship but twenty thousand gold ducats destined for the royal coffers when their caravel struck the shoals of Las Tibores. Twenty men survived the wreck in one boat without sails, water, or food and with only one set of oars. For two weeks they drifted, until they finally were caught in a current that carried them to the province of the Maya. Seven died on the journey; the rest were taken captive by a ruthless Cacique, who'd caged them and then sacrificed five of the castaways to his heathen idols and ate them.

Gerónimo and the others were being well fed for what they believed was a fattening up for the next savage fiesta. With luck, they'd managed to break out of their cage and escape, taking refuge with a chieftain named Aquincuz of the Xamananza. He was not on good terms with their original captor. But one by one the survivors had died, until only he and a seaman, one Gonzalo Guerrero, remained. Guerrero had refused to join him when he received Cortes's letter, as he had taken a rich native wife, painted his face and hands black in the native manner, and had many children by the woman. Gerónimo thought he was too ashamed to let his fellow countrymen see him in his new state. This did not matter to Cortes, for he had what he needed most in the person of Gerónimo, and now he was more determined than ever to set sail once again. But he would have to wait until the weather permitted.

Cortes's policy of making friends had turned the Indians of Cozumel into willing allies, eager to accept all the Spaniards said, even to taking up the god on the cross, along with his mother, as replacements for their own ancient, dark, and bloody lords of heaven. Through Gerónimo, he was able to preach the word of God to the heathens, as was his duty as a Christian soldier. The idols of Cozumel were cast down and destroyed by the Indians themselves, who worshiped before their new altars, burning incense and making small sacrifices of partridges, fruit, and maize but not the blood of humans.

From the time they had left Cuba, they'd spent nearly six weeks before they set sail to look for their still missing ship. With Cortes and Casca on the same brigantine, they searched the rivers and coves of the mainland, working their way slowly northward. Their efforts were rewarded when they reached a lagoon they called Puerto Escondido. There they found their lost vessel, unharmed and with its crew safe.

Cortes was not going to waste any more time now that he had his stray sheep. He ordered the fleet to set sail immediately. Juan watched as Casca stood on the bow of the flagship looking over the deep green waters. An old scar on his chest started to ache. He wondered what they would find when they reached the coast, where the Indians of Cozumel said the greatest of the kings held sway. His chest burned, though it had been centuries since he had lain upon the pyramid altar waiting for the sacrificial knife to descend. He shivered with the evening chill, his skin tingling from the spray splashing lightly over the bow. He had promised the people of the city of Teotihuacan that he would return one day, not really believing it. But now he *was* coming back. Was he still remembered as a god? Did his death mask of jade still rest in the sacred chamber of the pyramid temple, beneath the sign of the Feathered Serpent Quetzalcoatl? He had been the god, Quetza when he had left them after killing the monstrous king of the Olmecs, Teypeytel, named for the huge spotted cat that looked much like the leopards of Africa. The Feathered Serpent had been taken as a symbol from the dragon-prowed long ships with their red and white striped sails. He and his Nordic warriors had arrived in the tropic climes on such ships. His curse of life had for once been of benefit. When he had survived the plunge of the sacrificial dagger, the Teotecs believed him to be a god, and his word became law.

The only law he had given them was that human sacrifice would end. His memory cast back to that distant time when he had stood before the boy king of the Teotec, Cuzmecli, saying: "Your Majesty, wise men of the Teotec nation, listen to my words and pay heed. It has come to me that my time with you is at an end. The circle is complete. As I came to you from the sea, so I must return again to the sea. It is my fate and the will of the gods." The young boy king had started to protest against his leaving, but Casca had stopped him. "No, young king, it must be so. Now hear me. As I have said, everything is a great circle, and all that was shall be again. So it shall. One day I will return. Watch for me to come from the sea. I brought you messages from the gods. Obey them. There shall be no more human sacrifices on your altars. Remove from all the paintings and artwork of your city any sign of human sacrifice. It is not needed."

An aged shaman of the people had been nodding, when suddenly his eyes snapped open, a far, glazed look passing over the film-covered orbs. In a thin cracking voice he spoke:

"Tectli," he began, giving Casca the title due a noble. "I have seen that what you say is true. You will come again with others, but the ships will not be of the dragon. They will have many sails, and the men will appear different, with skins of shining light. Marvelous beasts will do their bidding and carry them into battle so that they will appear to be half man and half animal, able to run like the wind and travel far. They will spread fire and death among those who still sacrifice on the altars. The people of the valley will be destroyed, but they will not be our people. Our city will long since have been covered by the forests and deserts. But though our city will die, so shall those who come after us, because your laws will be broken.

"You shall return to the valley of the Teotec, but we shall be gone. Yet shall you be remembered. We shall send out holy men to tell of your law and your coming. As you have said, the circle will be complete, and those who have not honored your command will perish. As a people and a nation, they shall be as dust. New ones will inherit all that was in the valley. On 1 Reed, Tectli. It is so, and shall be . . ."

Casca snapped back from his reverie, the long-dead shaman's words haunting him. On 1 Reed he had said that Casca would return. He knew that by their calendar 1 Reed occurred every fifty-two years. Was this the time? The old priest had been right about him returning in ships with many sails, and there was little doubt that the wondrous beasts he had spoken of were the horses of the Spaniards. If the rest of the priest's vision was as accurate, there surely would be rivers of blood set loose upon the land before he left these shores again.

If Juan de Castro had been able to see what his friend had been dreaming of, he would have thought him a man gone mad. For him it was enough that he was part of this magnificent adventure, and his thoughts, while not as bloody-minded as some, still clung to the riches they might find and take home, riches enough to make them all kings. Casca didn't have to wonder what his young friend was thinking about. He knew the signs all too well and only hoped that cruel death, instead of gold and silver, did not wait for his gallant companion.

CHAPTER SIX

At a river the Indians called Tabasco, the ships of the fleet dropped anchor. The place looked familiar to Casca. He was certain that he had been there before and that this was to be the beginning of the old priest's prophecies. He had returned.

Many Indians had gathered on the shore to watch the anchoring of the fleet. They were well-built, handsome men who showed no overt sign of fear at the arrival of the Spaniards. They had seen ships similar to those of Cortes when Juan de Grijalba had anchored in these same waters, though he had not set foot on shore.

Cortes took the brigantine and a few of the ship's small boats loaded with men and several pieces of artillery up the river half a league, reaching a large city inside a wall of logs. It was filled with adobe houses roofed with straw. As they approached, several of the native boats, called *tahacups*, filled with warriors and set out to meet the Spaniards. The Indians seemed ready to fight. Casca watched over Cortes's shoulder, taking a long look at the men paddling toward them. Their faces were painted in whorls and circles of scarlet and black. They were armed with bows and light spears.

Cortes spoke to them through Gerónimo de Aquilar, offering them friendship, saying only that they wished to trade for food and water. The warriors in the *tahacups* said that they would take the strangers' words to their chief and return with his answer. Casca was still pleased that Cortes appeared to be behaving in a most gentle and conciliatory manner toward the Indians they met. Perhaps Cortes would be able to put the lie to the visions of the old priest. He hoped so.

In a short time, the Indians returned in their dugouts, bringing cakes of flat bread, fruit, and turkeys. These they offered as a gift from their chief. Cortes argued that what they had brought was too little for the number of mouths he had to feed and asked for permission to enter the city walls to buy more food. The Indians refused him, saying that they would return in the morning with word as to whether he would be permitted to land.

Cortes took his men to a small island in the center of the river to wait. While he was there, the Indians took all their goods and hid them, along with their women and children, in the woods. Cortes landed all his men with their matchlock arquebuses and crossbows on the island and then sent a strong scouting party upriver to look for a crossing in the event they were denied access to the village from the river. He sent word back to the fleet for the soldiers on board to join him on the island. These he took with him to where his scouts had located a place where they could cross. The waters were only waist deep, and the current was not strong enough to drag down the heavily armed Spaniards.

Casca hoped that the waters they were crossing didn't hide any of the large crocodiles he knew lived in many of the rivers and waters of these lands. Through thick brush and trees, they were able to get near the town without being detected by the Indians, who thought the Spaniards were still on the island. Cortes had left behind enough men in sight of the Indians' side of the river to make them think that all the men they had seen earlier were still there. He left two of his captains, Alonso de Avila and Pedro de Alvarado, with fifty men each. They were concealed in the brush with orders to make no sound or fires. They would be in a good position to attack the town from the land side if the Indians proved hostile to them and their demands.

The night was uneventful, the only activity being the endless droning of mosquitos and gnats, which did their best to make

the new arrivals welcome. With dawn, eight of the *tahacups*
came toward them. The warriors in them were armed more
heavily than those of the preceding day. Cortes didn't like the
looks of it but was determined to put on a good face for them.

The Indians stopped short of bow range from the Spaniards
on the island and cried out for them to accept what they had
been given and go home. There was nothing more for them in
these lands. Cortes responded with arguments, asking them to
reconsider. If they did, the Spaniards would show them how
much they could bring to the Indians. The leader of those in
the *tahacups* cried out: "We have no need of advice from such
as you. You are not welcome here. We do not trust you or
want anything from you. If you want water, dig wells for it as
we have. If you want food, hunt for it on the other side of the
river as we have. From us you will receive nothing."

Cortes took on a firmer attitude once he saw that smooth
words would not have any effect on his unwilling hosts. This
was the first time Casca had seen him act in this light. He rose
to his full height, pointing the tip of his fine Toledo blade at
the leader of the Indians: "I will not be denied that which I
have asked for in a reasonable manner. I have been sent here
by the greatest king on earth to explore and bring to the
savages the word of the living God. I wish only that which is
good for you. But if you refuse me in this matter, I will put
myself and those of my company in the hands of our god to
accomplish our divine purpose."

The Indian in the canoe only replied, "I care not for you or
your gods. We have strong gods of our own. Leave us and go
to a weaker people with your demands. You will not be permitted to enter our country or our city. If you try, we shall kill
you and all your men."

Cortes tried once more to reason with them, but he was
mocked by the Indians, who laughed at him and his offers to
save their immortal souls. He was getting peeved at the Indians' unreasonable attitudes, and he ended his entreaties
with: "I will give you till sundown to accept us as friends and
admit me to your city. If you refuse, then I shall, with the help
of God, sleep in your town this night in spite of you. Whatever
the cost is to you and your people will be on your head."

The vision of the priest of the Teotec seemed suddenly to be
much closer. There would be bloodshed.

Near sunset, when the Indians made no attempt to contact

them again, Cortes alerted his men who were hidden in the brush to prepare themselves for battle. He donned his armor, put his shield on his arm, and then, calling upon God, Saint Peter, and Saint James, beached the brigantine by the wall nearest the shore, landed the artillery, and began his assault on the walls with two hundred men.

The Indians fired at them with their stone-tipped arrows and light lances, doing little damage to the armored soldiers of Castile. Twenty-two were wounded, but none of the injuries were of a fatal or even crippling nature. The noise and smoke of the cannons confused and frightened the Indians more than anything else. They didn't know how to deal with such a thing. Many simply went to their knees and began praying to their gods to save them, though most continued to fight bravely. The sound of the cannons was the signal for those in hiding among the trees and brush to begin their assault from the rear of the village.

Casca and Juan were in the first line of soldiers that clambered over the stockade walls, using ropes and ladders they had brought for that purpose. They met little resistance; their steel blades sliced through the wicker and skin shields of the Indians as if they weren't there. More than once an Indian simply held up his hands to await the death that was coming after he'd struck a Spaniard full in the chest with an obsidian-lined ax, only to see it bounce off the steel breastplate of his bearded foe. When the Indians turned to meet the new attack from their rear, they had to take men away from the wall Cortes was attacking. With that, Cortes had little difficulty breaching the walls. The Spanish forces had the Indians between them and began pushing them to the city square like the jaws of a vise, drawing ever tighter.

Juan got a bit too eager and overconfident. He rushed a knot of painted, howling warriors, attempting to beat them back by himself. His sword took out two of them before they swarmed over him, dragging him down, trying to peel him out of his breastplate. If Casca hadn't been keeping an eye on him, he might have gained fame by being the first Spaniard killed in the Cortes expedition. Slashing the throat of one Indian with his sword, Casca slashed at the others until they ran shrieking from the battle, convinced they'd been fighting devils instead of men.

When the two forces met, it was more of a slaughter than a

battle as they finished off the surviving warriors, who had
already resigned themselves to their fate. Fewer than thirty of
the Indian warriors were able to escape into the woods. The
rest, numbering nearly four hundred, were killed or taken
prisoner.

After the prisoners had been secured, the village was
searched, but to Cortes's displeasure, they found no sign of
gold or treasure. The Spaniards, except for those who now
guarded the walls, followed Cortes into the temple grounds.
The idols there were destroyed, and the Spaniards took over
the temple as their headquarters. It provided the most room
and was the strongest building in the village in case of a
counterattack by the hostile Indians. Cortes, true to his word,
slept in the village that night, and his stay was most definitely
at the expense of the Indians. The conquistadors had fought
and won their first battle. There were more attempts made by
Cortes to open the lines of communication with the chief of
the region by releasing many of his captives, but this did no
good. As a result, there was some minor fighting over the next
few days as the rest of the Spaniards, along with the horses
and six cannon, were offloaded and brought into the village.
The ships remained anchored at a safe distance with enough
men to ward off any attack, which Cortes didn't think likely.
The Tabascans, as could be seen from their ill-made canoes,
were not fond of the sea beyond their harbors. There were a
few skirmishes during this time, in which many minor wounds
were received by the Spaniards, but still there were no
fatalities.

Cortes was confident that he had taught the Tabascans a
lesson they would not soon forget. In this he was mistaken.
The Tabascans sent word to all their tribes to send warriors to
drive back the invaders. Eight thousand answered the call. The
Spaniards used horses to scout the countryside, and it wasn't
long before the movement of so many warriors was discovered. Cortes had no desire to fight from a static position
behind the walls of the village, where the attrition rate would
be in the favor of the Tabascans. Once he was fairly certain of
the enemy's position, he formed his small army and set out for
the village of Cintla, where some of his men had been am-
bushed earlier. By the time they arrived, the Tabascans had
formed their army and waited for the arrival of the Spaniards.

Juan stayed with the infantry, and Casca was sent with the cavalry on the left flank, following Cortes as he attempted to lead them around to the rear of the Indians. He would go through the woods and come in behind them. Cortes placed the rest of the men and cannon where they'd have a fair field of fire across the cultivated fields that were to be their battleground. The terrain was not very good, crisscrossed with canals and ditches, but there was no other place for it. The Tabascans didn't wait very long before they threw themselves on the Spaniards. The sheer weight of their numbers forced the Castilians back.

It was the horses that saved the day. When the cavalry made its appearance at the rear of the Tabascans, they broke in terror, thinking that the strange creatures attacking them were half man and half beast. With only thirteen horsemen, Cortes was able to force the Indians out into a more open spot where the lances of the cavalry did good and bloody duty. The screaming of the war-horses frightened the Indians more than the thunder of the cannon. Once the pressure was off the Spanish infantry, they were able to join the fray, adding to the flight of the Tabascans with their crossbows and arquebuses. The heavy bolts from the crossbows went through the Indians' puny shields as if they weren't there, and the wounds were such as they had never seen, tearing out great chunks of meat, blasting chests open, ripping off faces and heads from their bodies.

This, with the devil beasts trampling them, was too much. The Tabascans broke, leaving over three hundred dead behind them. Seventy-three Spaniards were wounded, but again none were killed. Casca wondered how long their luck could hold up. He knew the effect that not being able to kill any of the Spaniards was going to have on the primitive Tabascans.

The Spanish wounded were taken into the city of Cintla and treated. The prisoners taken from the Tabascans were herded into the temple grounds in the center of the town. By Cortes's orders, they were also given aid for their wounds and treated with courtesy. In the morning he released five nobles and allowed them to return to their chiefs. They carried another message from him, saying: "I regret that mistrust and ill fortune have caused me to do such harm. Though I swear by my god, it was not of my doing, but your own. Yet if you will come to me, I will forgive you and make peace. If you do not come within two days, I shall have no other choice but to ravage your lands and burn your cities. As you have seen in our battles, you have not been able to kill even one of my soldiers. Yet hundreds of your warriors lie dead or have been taken prisoner. Come to me within two days or all of your men shall die. Come to me and I shall reveal great mysteries to you, and you shall be the better for my coming."

The freed captives delivered the messages to their chiefs, who after council sent fifty nobles to speak to the Spaniards. They asked for permission to take their dead away and the promise of safe conduct for their chiefs if they came to speak to the chief of the Spaniards. This was granted with the warning that they not repeat their acts of treachery or their chiefs would meet with certain death, bringing great tragedy to their country.

The Tabascans had made the proper sacrifices before the battle at Cintla. They had given the gods the hearts of brave men to feed upon. They had made, as was right and proper, manstew of the flesh of the victims, sharing it among the eight thousand warriors to give them the courage of those braves who had been chosen as heavenly messengers. This had done them no good. They had fought bravely, but who could be expected to stand against men whose shining armor stopped the fiercest of blows, men who had the thunder of the heavens at their command, able to spit death and fire at their enemies, and most terrifying of all, the beasts with the two heads—the deerlike creature who screamed, pawing the earth, outrunning their fastest man as if he were a crippled child. The chieftains of the Tabascans were all in agreement that the gods of their fathers had deserted them and that the power of these newcomers was such that they could not be resisted any longer. They would go to the chief of the bearded men, asking for the mercy he had promised.

At the end of the time set by Cortes, the chiefs of the Tabascans made their appearance before the gates of what once had been one of their cities to ask permission to enter and parley with the chief of the strangers from the sea. With them they brought food, turkeys, maize, fruits, and other edibles. They also had with them twenty female slaves to do the cooking and grinding of maize for the Spaniards. In addition, there were a few small items of gold and turquoise which the Spanish valued at not more than two or three hundred pesos. It was certainly not anything like the treasure they had come after. Cortes still believed that great wealth was to be found—if not here, then elsewhere. From the Tabascans he questioned, he learned of another, greater kingdom where they said there was gold and silver to fill rivers. The land was ruled by a great king with warriors at his command like the grains of sand on the beach. It was a nation of warriors who ruled over a hundred vassal tribes that paid them tribute. If they went to the land of the Aztecs ruled by the priest king Moctezuma, they would find what they sought.

From the directions they gave, Casca was certain of the prophecy, for the Tabascans had described the lakes and the valley near the city of Teotihuacan. He was returning!

Although the Tabascans were not on the best of terms with their neighbors, it was the scarcity of gold in Tabasco that convinced Cortes the Indians were telling him the truth, though the former would have been the more logical reason. For the Tabascans had to buy peace from the Aztecs by providing them with victims for Aztec altars.

The monks with Cortes went about their job of saving the souls of the heathen and bringing them to Jesus, whose power was greater than that of the Indians' multitude of gods. The victory of the Spaniards over the Tabascan army made the conversions easy, and the idols of Tabasco were cast down and replaced with the symbol of the cross. Cortes was being very careful to keep the Church on his side in this expedition. He knew that his enemies in Cuba would move against him one day, especially if he found that which he truly sought—the great wealth of an unknown world.

Cortes didn't delay; he gave the orders to set sail for the river named after its discoverer, the Alvarado, which the Indians called the Papaloapan. Up the river, they would come to the first of the cities inhabited by the Aztecs. There they would find gold, silver, precious stones, and, what many of the Tabascans hoped for, *death*.

The Alvarado was wide and deep, the banks dripping with heavy foliage and wild with animal life. There were birds of many kinds: cormorants, gulls, black ducks with white wings valued by the natives for their feathers and white herons called god-birds, or *teoquechal*. The waters held sea lions and shad the size of tuna. A strange large lizard with a spiked body and four toes could be found swimming or climbing trees. Its flesh tasted like that of a rabbit and was much favored by the Spaniards once they had a sample of it. Pigs, deer, monkeys, puma—all were seen on the banks of the river. There was one strange little beast that fascinated the Spaniards, for they had never seen anything even remotely resembling it in Spain or Cuba. The Indian slave women with them said it was called the *ayotochli*, meaning pumpkin rabbit. It was the size of a large cat, with the face of a duck, the feet of a porcupine, and a long tail. It was covered with hard plates that fit together like a suit of armor, which the beast would curl up in when threatened. The Spaniards named it the "armored one," *el armadillo*.

CHAPTER SEVEN

Moctezuma was again troubled by dreams. The year 13 Rabbit would soon end, and then it would be 1 Reed. He ordered his chamberlain, the *petlacatl*, to bring him all the wizards and men of magic he could find from the villages around Tenochtitlán. Once this was done, he asked them if they had not seen the signs in the skies or had dreams and visions of strange things to come. None of them admitted to those experiences. At this response, he commanded that they be locked up in the prison of Cuauhcalco, where they would remain until they gave him a more agreeable answer. In the morning, he ordered his chamberlain to question them again, demanding that they tell him if sickness, famine, or drought was to come upon the land. He also asked whether war or strange deaths would occur and whether they had heard the voice of Cihuacoatl, the weeping goddess who was often heard to cry out in the night when danger threatened.

His chamberlain returned. Bowing before his lord, he gave him the answer of the wizards, who had replied: "What can we say? The future has already been decreed in heaven. Moctezuma will see and suffer a great mystery, which must come to pass in the land of the Aztecs. If the great king wishes to know more, he will learn soon enough, for it comes swiftly.

This is what we prophesy. Since the king demands that we speak, and since it must surely take place, we can only wait for it to come.''

Moctezuma became extremely agitated, for their predictions were nearly the same as those he had received earlier from Nezahualpilli, king of Texcoco, who was widely famed as a man of great visions. He ordered his chamberlain, "Return to the prison once more and ask the wizards if the mystery is to come by land, sea, or air, and when it will happen."

When the *petlacatl* returned to the prison, he found that the wizards were all gone. The cells were empty, and the guards swore that they had heard and seen nothing. Terrified, he returned to Moctezuma. Throwing himself on his face before his master, he cried out: "My lord, command that I be cut to pieces, or do what you will with me, for you must know that when I arrived at the prison and opened the doors, no one was there. The guards are all good and loyal men who have served me for years, but none of them heard the wizards escape. I believe they flew away, using their magic to make themselves invisible, which, as it is well known, is within the powers of such as they.''

Moctezuma had no desire to punish one loyal to him. He said, "Let them go. Call the chiefs together and give them my order to go to the villages of the magicians. They are to kill their wives and all their children and then destroy their houses.'' The chiefs did as they were bade, killing the women by hanging them with ropes and the children by smashing them against the walls of their homes. Then the houses were torn down and the foundations uprooted.

Three days later a *macehual* (a common man) came from Mictla near the coast. He had seen something that he had to tell the king of. He went directly to Moctezuma's palace and was lucky enough to be able to speak to the chamberlain, who quickly showed him into the presence of the king of the Aztecs. Moctezuma gave the man, who had no ears or toes— they had been cut off as punishment for some minor offense —permission to speak.

"Oh my lord and king, forgive me for daring to come to you. I am from Mictla. When I went to the shores by the sea, there was a small mountain floating in the midst of the water, moving here and there without touching the shore. My lord, we have never seen the likes of this before, although we guard the coast and are always on watch."

Moctezuma thanked him for his message and then told his chamberlain to take the man to the prison and hold him under careful guard till his story could be confirmed. After they had gone, he called for a *tuectlama-cazqui*, a priest of his order called Tez-cuzcli, and appointed him his emissary, charging him: "Go to Cuetlaxtlan. Tell the official in charge of the village that it is true that strange things have appeared on the sea. He is to investigate these things himself. Tell him to make all haste in this matter so that I may determine what it is they signify. And take with you the ambassador, Cuitlapitoc, to assist you and add weight to your words."

When the priest and Cuitlapitoc arrived in Cuetlaxtlan, they were taken to a man named Pinotl, who was the magistrate for the region. He listened to the words with great care, for they came from the lips of his king who had power over all things. Then he replied: "My lords, rest here with me and send your servants out to the shore."

The attendants did as they were ordered and returned in great haste to report that the story told by the *macehual* was true. They had seen two great towers or small mountains floating on the waves of the sea.

Cuitlapitoc told Pinotl: "I wish to see these things myself in order to learn what they are, for I must testify to our lord as an eyewitness. I will be satisfied with this and will report to him exactly that which I see."

The priest Tez-cuzcli accompanied Cuitlapitoc, for he could do no less than the other in this mission. When they reached the shore, they hid in the branches of a tree and looked out over the ocean. They saw that seven of the strangers had left the floating mountains and were fishing from a small boat with lines and hooks. They watched the fishermen until they returned to their mother ship and set sail, heading back to the open sea. They made careful note of all they witnessed. When they returned to the village, they made a hasty departure to return to Tenochtitlán to report what they had seen to their lord.

Moctezuma had not slept two hours in a row since they had left. His eyes were hollow-looking, even under the black eye paint he wore.

"Our lord and king, it is true," began Tez-cuzcli. "There are strange men who have come to our shores from the great sea. They were fishing from a small boat, some with rods, others with nets. They fished until late, then returned to what I am sure is not a mountain or tower but a monster boat such as has never been dreamed of. There were many others like those who were fishing. Some wore jackets of blue, green, and red; others wore a drab, soiled-looking garment like our *ictilmatli* (the peasant's cloak of woven maguey fibers). On their heads they wore scarves of red or hats of fine scarlet color. They are very light in color. Many have hair that is the color of grain, though some have black. Most seem to have long beards. These too are of the color of ripe grain. However, lord, they have gone away, back to the seas whence they came. This is all that we have seen, lord, this and no more."

Moctezuma was silent. His fears were coming true. Strangers from the sea had come to Mexico. They would be back, for it was not yet 1 Reed.

The king of the Aztecs was silent for a long moment. The servants kneeling before him were anxious, not knowing whether their words had pleased their lord. Moctezuma's face trembled; the muscles rippled along the side of his jaw as he tried to regain control of his emotions.

"You are the chiefs of my own house and palace. I place more trust and faith in you than anyone else, because you have always told me the truth. Go with the *petlacatl*. Bring me the man who is locked up in the prison, the *macehual* who came as a messenger from the coast."

They bowed away from his presence to do his bidding, going to the prison, where they found that the common man too somehow had escaped with no trace.

When they related this event to their king, Moctezuma became very agitated. The tic along his jaw beat as if it had a thrice-fast pulse of its own. It was difficult for him to control the fear in his voice at this new wonder. He told his terrified chiefs, "It is a natural thing, for I am certain that he too was a wizard. But hear now what I say, and if you reveal anything of what I am about to command, I will bury you under my halls. Your wives and children will be killed and your property seized; your homes will be destroyed to the bottom of their foundations. Your parents and all your kin will be put to death. I believe that what you have witnessed are the advance guard of the Quetza. He will return, but not for some months. In this time we must prepare for his arrival. Send messages to all our cities and those of our vassals that when the strangers return, they are to be treated as honored guests. Let no harm be done them or any threats made to them. Give them gifts and slaves in my name."

The next months were an agony of anticipation. It was a relief when at last a messenger dropped before him bearing a scroll from Tuedilli, the governor of Cotstala, near where the first ships had been sighted. His message read: "My lord, I have done as you ordered. The strangers have been made welcome in your name and gifts and slaves given them to make their stay more pleasant. On this scroll see that I have shown the number of their monstrous canoes and the strangeness of their countenance. I will show them all honor pending your further instructions."

Moctezuma was in a sweaty lather as he summoned his chamberlain and Tez-cuzcli to his presence, telling them of the letter from Tuedilli: "I told you they would return. Now bring me two of the finest artists among the silversmiths and two from those who are skillful at the working of emeralds and turquoise."

This was done, and Moctezuma gave the artists his commands, ordering them to make haste, for he had much to do, and the dark gods were restless.

The king didn't sleep for the next three days. His eyes were dark hollows; worry lines etched their marks across his brow. He looked much older than he had in the past week. He was afraid to sleep; too many dark, troubled things came to haunt his mind when his eyes closed even for a moment. It was a great relief when he was informed by one of his palace hunchbacks that the artisans had finished their assignments. Not waiting for them to be brought to him, he hurried to the work place that had been given them in the palace. The senior of the craftsmen bowed to his lord, the large silver bars in his ears swaying with the bobbing of his head. He said, "Our lord, the work is finished. Please inspect it."

He indicated a large table on which the articles Moctezuma had ordered to be made were laid out for his approval: throat bands of gold with links four fingers wide, each link set with emeralds from the south, matching earrings beside it, gold bracelets with chains of gold hanging from them; double bracelets for both ankles and wrists, each set with emeralds; two fans of rich feathers, in the center of one side, a half moon of gold, on the other, a golden sun; and many, many other fine rich works from the hands of the Aztec craftsmen.

Moctezuma was pleased, saying to his chamberlain and the *petlacatl*, "My grandfathers, give each of these men a portion of rich cloths and quills filled with gold dust and seed of every kind. Give them cloth for their women, the same amount to each." The artisans left, feeling very well rewarded for their labors, knowing that the favor of the king could have easily turned to disfavor, costing them their lives if they had not pleased him.

Moctezuma was certain that the legend was coming true; there was no doubt in his mind. There had been too many signs and portents. He had to make the gods welcome to avoid their displeasure and the disasters that would surely follow if he didn't. The articles he had ordered were only to be a part of the gifts he would send by special emissaries to the strangers from the sea. If he was wrong and they were only mortal men, the mistake could be remedied by the sacrifice of their beating hearts to the god of war. In the meantime, he had to be careful not to offend them. The gifts he sent must be of the finest to show how he honored them.

Five messengers were to escort the treasure and see it safely to the strangers. They were led by the senior priest of the sanctuary of Yohualican and nobles from Tepoztlan, Mictlan, Huehuetlan, and Tizatlan. They were all members of his own clans and knights of the Jaguar Order.

To these loyal men he said, "Come closer, my nobles of the Jaguar, come closer. It is said that the god has returned from the sea to our land. Go to him, hear him. Listen well to what he says to you; listen and remember all.

"You will have charge of the gifts I am sending." He showed them what had been prepared so that they would know the importance he placed on their mission. "First is the treasure of the god Quetzalcoatl." There was a serpent mask inlaid with turquoise, a collar of rare quetzal feathers with a gold sun in the center, a shield inlaid with mother-of-pearl and gold bordered with the matching feathers, and a pendant of the same pattern and make. He touched the serpent mask reverently with one jeweled finger. There was another mask of the god Quetzalcoatl kept in the pyramid temple dedicated to him by the lake's edge. That mask did not bear any likeness to the serpent but to the strange man with a scar running from the corner of his eye to his mouth. It was said to be the exact likeness of the god, made for him when he walked the earth giving his law. Of course, that did not mean that the god would have to look the same when he returned. A god obviously could take on any aspect he wished.

The rest of the finery dedicated to the serpent god consisted of a diadem of jaguar skin and pheasant feathers, earrings of turquoise, and jade cloaks bordered with small gold bells. There was also a golden shield and the crooked staff of Ehecatl, who was the Quetzalcoatl in his aspect as the god of winds; for the winds came from the seas as came the god who rode upon them.

Moctezuma showed his emissaries the remaining gifts that had been handcrafted, and these, together with many other gifts of gold and precious stones, he gave into their charge, saying to them with great seriousness, "Go now and do not tarry. Go with the noble Tuedilli and pay reverence to our lord Quetzalcoatl. Say to him, 'Moctezuma, your deputy, has sent us to you. Here are the presents with which he welcomes you home to Mexico.'"

Moctezuma returned to his chambers, where his guards were ordered to admit no one. They too were of the Jaguar Order. Their shields bore five soft tufts of eagle down to symbolize their trusted status.

At last satisfied that he had done all that he could, Moctezuma slept upon his couch and dreamed of a scar-faced man who rode through his land on a strange beast. He left death and destruction all about him, but there was a great sadness on the timeless face.

The king slept uneasily this night, for it was 1 Reed....

CHAPTER EIGHT

The Spanish at last dropped their anchors in a sheltered cove to the west of the lands of the Tabascans. The anchors had scarcely touched water before several canoes from the shore were putting out to meet them. Aquilar had trouble understanding much of their language, but through signs they were able to make it known that the chief of the region, one Tuedilli, wished to make them welcome. In his usual politic manner, Cortes treated the emissaries well. Showing great courtesy and honor, he brought them on board his flagship, not only to make them welcome but also to impress them with the strength of the Spaniards. Wine was given them, which they found good in comparison with the throat-searing pulque they were used to. They were given several small gifts, which they immediately took to Tuedilli, a small, dark man with large golden hoops set in his earlobes. He had his orders from Moctezuma and would obey them to the letter. The visitors would be treated as nobles and honored guests.

The next day, on Good Friday, Cortes set foot in the empire of the Aztecs. He had the heavy guns and horses offloaded as well. He knew that he had to establish his presence in an authoritative manner when dealing with savages.

Casca went with the advance party, helping to select the best campsite among the dunes lining the beach. He was starting to regret his decision to return to these alien lands. A sour taste began to settle in the back of his mouth. He was the only one of the company who had any knowledge of the capabilities of the people the Spaniards were treating with such disdain. He knew that beyond their sight lay great cities that would rival any of the capitals that the kings of Europe ruled over.

The two hundred Cuban Indians they had brought with them as servants quickly cleared an area for a campsite, using the trees and brush along the shore to build huts to house the Spaniards and their equipment. It was but an hour before Indians from the nearby villages began to come in to see the strangers. Quickly, a thriving barter system was established. The Indians traded articles of gold for glass beads, which they thought to be jewels, and mirrors, which they prized highly. When they returned to their villages, it was with the feeling that they had by far gotten the best in their dealings with the Spaniards. By the next day, enough food had been traded so that the immediate needs of supplying Cortes's army was not any great problem. He did give one order, though. None of his men could barter for gold privately. He didn't want to take a chance on letting the natives see how greatly they prized it at this moment. That would best be saved for later.

On the morning of Easter Sunday, Tuedilli, the chief of the area and a noble of the Eagle Clan, came from Costastla, escorted by four thousand men. He was making a personal visit to his uninvited guests in accordance with the orders of Moctezuma. In order to show his friendliness, none of the four thousand with him came armed. Of the escort, six hundred were nobles of varying ranks, the rest were either slaves or servants to the nobles. The Spaniards were impressed with the dignity of the Aztecs in addition to the richness of their clothing, much of it made of cleverly woven feathers or fine cotton, decorated with pins and ornaments of silver and gold and set with precious stones.

Tuedilli disliked the look of the Spaniards, with their hairy faces and pale skins, but orders were orders. He bowed to their leader and then made a small cut on his arm with a silver dagger. He dipped straws into his own blood to present to the captain of the Spaniards as a symbol of honor. Gifts were given. This time they were of greater value than the small things they had traded for with the Indians. These were easily recognized as works of art of great worth. Copal incense was burned to bring good spirits to the meeting. All this was done in the name of Moctezuma. In exchange, Cortes gave to Tuedilli a coat of silk, a medallion bearing the likeness of Saint James, several strings of glass beads, which the Aztecs once again thought were jewels, looking glasses, scissors, and many small items of iron, wool, and leather. The Aztecs handled each gift as if it were priceless. They carefully wrapped and placed each item in a separate basket to be carried back to Costastla individually.

The difficult parts of the transactions and initial greetings were made without the services of Aquilar, who simply could not grasp the dialect of the Aztec nobles.

Casca noticed one of the slave girls given to them by the Tabascans talking with one of the Aztec slaves. She was a pretty girl in her twenties with dark eyes and thick black hair tied in a knot. Her features had a clean, intelligent look. Taking her by the arm, he brought her to Cortes. This was the first time he'd spoken directly to the leader of the expedition. He had been very careful on this trip to make no friends. He simply did his job and kept out of everyone's way.

Moving up close to Cortes, he spoke softly: "Señor, I believe this woman has a grasp of the tongue of these Aztecs. Perhaps through Aquilar and her, you would be able to communicate with them better."

Cortes eyed the man speaking to him. There was a strangely quiet quality to him. A weariness that was not of the body lay behind a scarred, beardless face. He had noticed the man before, but there had been no reason to speak to him directly. "*Gracias*, señor." He waited for the man to give him his name.

"Romano, my captain, Carlos Romano."

Cortes stroked his spade-shaped beard thoughtfully with a forefinger. "It is good to have men who use their wits in my company. If it is as you have said, then truly this woman may be of great value to us in communicating with the savages. Find Aquilar and send him to me that I may see if she is capable of serving our purpose. Then I would have speech with you. Come to me at my tent after sundown."

Leaving the scar-faced man to find Aquilar, Cortes indi-

cated that Tuedilli and his lords should accompany some of
the Spanish officers on a tour of the camp, with a special em-
phasis on showing them the horses and cannon. Taking the
woman gently by the arm, he led her to his tent, where he tried
to reassure her by his manner that she was not in any trouble
or danger.

Aquilar showed up a few minutes later. He looked much
better than when he had first come to them. His face had filled
out, and he was regaining much of the confidence he had lost
while a prisoner of the Indians of Yucatan. Cortes asked him
to speak to the woman and find out how good her knowledge
of the Aztec tongue was. He leaned back against his cot while
the two conversed for a few minutes.

Aquilar turned to his leader. He said, "She says that she has
a good grasp of the language, having learned to speak it as a
child. She is well educated for one from these lands. Her
parents were wealthy merchants, but she was stolen by slavers
some years ago and eventually ended up in the hands of the
Tabascans. Her own village, Oluta, is not far from those of
the Aztecs, and they have much in common in the way of
speech and customs. She has also been converted to the true
faith by the good fathers and has been given the name of
Marina to replace that given to her at birth."

Cortes was pleased by the information. He told Aquilar to
tell her that if she served him faithfully, she would be well
rewarded. She would not have to do any more of the woman's
work or bed any of his soldiers unless she wanted to.

Once Cortes was certain of the girl's capabilities, he gave
orders for the Aztec nobles to be seated in a semicircle. He was
seated in the center with Tuedilli on his right. Food was prepared and served by the Cubans as Cortes, through Aquilar
and then Marina, told the chieftain of his mission: "Lords and
guests, I am the emissary of the greatest king on earth, Don
Carlos of Austria, king of Spain, emperor of the Christians,
and lord of lands more vast than the Aztecs could dream of."

He leaned closer to Tuedilli, trying to read any expression
behind the dark eyes, watching the body for signs that might
give him a clue as to the effect his words were having. Tuedilli
kept a bland expression on his face. His hands were steady,
but his heart began to pound a bit. Cortes noticed the pulse at
the temple of the chief's head becoming more pronounced.

His words were having an effect.

After clearing his throat with a small taste of wine, he continued: "My lord Tuedilli, my master is a king who is served by kings and princes who rejoice in obeying his commands, for he is good and wise above all others. He has heard of your land and its great lord and has commanded me to come here as his ambassador to bring words that are for his ears only. Great secrets shall I give to your king." Cortes touched Tuedilli's arm, pleased to feel a light sheen of nervous sweat in the fine, dark hairs of the Aztec's forearm. "I have given you my master's message; now, when can I expect to be received by your master, the noble Moctezuma?"

Tuedilli listened to the words of Cortes through the mouth of Marina. But they were not the exact words that Cortes had spoken, for Marina had translated them in the manner she thought would serve the Spaniard best. She knew what was in the minds of the Aztecs from her earlier conversations with them. She knew the legend of the Quetza as well as they did. In her translation she left the impression that Cortes might be the god who was returning to his land. In her words, Don Carlos, the king, became the great god and Cortes one of his aspects.

Tuedilli was deeply concerned. He didn't want to make any moves that could mean his head. As a politician, he knew that the best thing he could do was to stall Cortes and wait for more orders. He said only that he was very glad to hear of the greatness and kindness of the lord emperor but that Cortes should know that his master was a great lord also, with kings who served him and warriors by the tens of thousands at his command. He would, as befitted a good servant, send the request to meet with Moctezuma to Moctezuma himself, as it was not his place to say that which his master should say.

After this exchange, Cortes gave the order for his troops to parade in mock battle. The savages needed to have a little Christian fear put into their souls. Horses charged, the steel blades of the Spaniards slicing through the air as they used their native shields for targets, cutting them to ribbons. A barricade of logs was erected at the far end of the field and used as a target for the combined fire of the cannon. The logs burst into splinters as the muzzles vomited thunder and flame. Then the horses nearly charged into the faces of the awestruck Aztecs, the men on the animals' backs crying out to Saint

James and the king. They wheeled their horses, spinning away only mere feet from the terrified Aztecs.

It was then that Cortes asked Tuedilli, "Does Moctezuma have much gold?"

Stunned, Tuedilli responded automatically: "Yes!"

Cortes grinned at the fear on his guest's face. "Then have him send me some of it, for my companions suffer from a sickness that can be cured only by gold." Cortes was at last revealing his true colors.

Marina whispered into the ear of Tuedilli: "Can you not see the gods have returned?" Tuedilli made a hasty apology for having to leave the company. He wanted to put some distance between himself and these terrible beings and monstrous implements of destruction. This would have to be reported immediately to the capital. Runners would be sent to Tenochtitlán, seventy leagues distant, and take with them the pictures drawn on cotton cloth of what he had witnessed. Then he would make sacrifices of his own to appease and gain the support of his gods. Before he left, he ordered two of his nobles to remain in the camp to see to the needs of the Spaniards. In their charge were two thousand Indians who had been drafted from the local tribes to be the servants of the Spaniards. Tuedilli now understood Moctezuma's fear of the strangers from the sea. If they were not gods, they still had powers not known to mortal men. He knew that Moctezuma would be troubled greatly by his message.

CHAPTER NINE

After Casca's meeting in the tent of Cortes, he came away impressed with the man's drive and absolute faith in his destiny. He'd told Casca to continue to use his brain since there might come a time when he would have need of an intelligent friend. Casca used this opening as an opportunity to ask Cortes for permission to use the services of Aquilar and Marina. From then on, he spent most of his time listening to the speech of the Aztecs, trying to reach back into the dim recesses of his memory for any familiar words. Some of the language struck distant chords, but what he really experienced was the half-familiar taste of something long forgotten. It was from Aquilar and Marina that he began to learn the rudiments of the speech the Aztecs called Nahual. For many days, even after the gifts of Moctezuma had come and been presented, he devoted most of his time to learning the things he would need to know. Marina told him of the Aztecs and their culture, how the place of lakes where their capital was had two names that were used interchangeably. The valley was called Mexico, which meant the source or the center. Its people were called either Aztec or Mexicas, as even Tenochtitlán was called the city of Mexico. This she had long since related to Cortes that he might not confused with the interchanging of titles.

Casca worked from dawn till dusk. If he wasn't pestering Aquilar or Marina, he was dragging a protesting Juan with him to visit with the Indians, making them show him different articles and their corresponding names in Nahual. He had always had the gift of tongues, and it served him well in his endless travels from one nation and culture to the next. He found that many of the words were becoming more familiar now. He learned much more quickly than Aquilar or even Marina could have expected. He had a purpose in his mind, and to accomplish it, he required the knowledge of a minimum amount of words. He had to learn whether the Aztecs were worth saving. He had seen the pure gleam of avarice in the eyes of the Spaniards when Tuedilli and his nobles had presented Cortes with their offerings from Moctezuma.

To Juan it was a bit boring. He couldn't understand why his friend went to such lengths to understand pagans. Casca had hoped that Juan would take an interest in the natives beyond their wealth in gold, but it was a futile exercise. The young Castilian was too much a victim of his own culture to accept another's right to exist.

When the gifts of Moctezuma arrived, it was clear to Cortes that he was close to that which he sought most of all—the wealth of a great nation. The ambassadors from Moctezuma came to his ships while the captain was on board. There they offered him straws dipped in their own blood, as Tuedilli had done the first time they'd met. Then they showed him the gifts and dressed him in the feathered robes of the Quetza, placing the serpent mask of blue-green turquoise over his face, with its gold earrings hanging down on either side. They put on his chest a vest and collar of *chalcuhuites*, with a gold sun disk in the center. On his hips they fastened mirrors of polished silver, and from his shoulders they hung a cloak known as the ringing bell. On his shins were placed greaves that were set with turquoise and emeralds. Attached to them were little bells of fine gold that rang as he walked. Into his hands they placed the shield with its gold center and fringe of cobalt feathers and ornaments of mother-of-pearl and gold. Last, they put his feet into black sandals made from the hide of the great lizards that swam in the waters of the rivers to the far south. When this was done, they laid the rest of their gifts before him for his pleasure and bowed their heads before the god. Cortes merely said: "Is this all? Is this the extent of your gifts of welccme? Is this how you greet me?"

From this, Casca knew that the Indians were in for a rough time. The other gifts given to them, which Cortes treated so poorly, consisted of two disks, one of the sun, weighing one hundred marks, the other of the moon, weighing fifty. The disks were each ten palms in diameter and thirty in circumference. A rough estimate of their value was twenty thousand ducats. The jewels and other items were probably worth as much. Forty thousand ducats would have paid for their trip ten times over. Yet it only served to whet the appetites of the Castilians. Once this sample had been seen, there was no stopping the Spaniards. They knew that the real treasure would have to be in the capital city of the Aztecs, and that was where they would go.

Once the gifts were accepted, Cortes gave the orders for the cannon on the ships to be fired. At their sound, the gift bearers from Moctezuma fainted in shock, for they had never heard anything like the thunder which came at the command of the god.

Once they had been revived with wine, Cortes removed his mask and said to them: "I have heard that the warrior of Mexico is a great fighter, brave at heart and terrible in battle, that he knows how to retreat, counter, and rush back to conquer, even if his enemy is ten or even twenty times his number. This I wish to see for myself. I want to find out if you are as brave and strong as your people say you are." With this he gave them shields of leather, native swords, and spears, dismissing them after saying: "On the morrow, at daybreak, we are going to fight each other in pairs. In this way we can learn the truth. We will see who falls to the ground!"

The ambassadors were terrified. This they had not expected. They said to Cortes through his interpreters, "Our lord, we were not sent here for this by Moctezuma! We have come on an exclusive mission to bring you his gifts, to offer you friendship and repose. What the lord desires is not within our warrant to give. If we did this thing, we might anger Moctezuma, who would surely order our deaths and those of our families."

Cortes was determined to humiliate them and fill their souls with awe at the might of the conquistadors. "No! It will be done. I must see for myself, because even in Castile they say you are famous as brave warriors. Therefore, eat an early meal. I will also eat. So be of good cheer!'' With this he let them leave the boats, knowing full well that they would not be found anywhere near his camp in the morning. They were not going to go against the wishes of their king, but he had achieved his purpose by proving the readiness of the Spaniards to fight.

To the amusement of those on the ships, when the ambassadors practically jumped into their canoes to paddle away, some of them took to using their hands to hasten their departure. Tez-cuzcli cried to his friends, ''Hurry, hurry, we must get away from here. Nothing must happen to us here. Nothing!''

The ambassadors reached Xicalanco in great haste, stopping only to eat and gather provisions. Then they raced on through one city after another, not stopping even to rest for the night when a village official offered them shelter. ''No!'' they replied hastily. ''We must keep going! We must report to the king all that we have seen, and it is a terrible thing. Nothing like this has ever been seen before!''

Now that he had seen a sample of the wealth of the Aztecs, Cortes would not allow anything to prevent him from reaching the source of the gold, the capital city of Mexico—Tenochtitlán. He attempted diplomacy again, requesting that Tuedilli send him with a proper escort to the capital. This Tuedilli refused, stating, ''Lord, the way is long and hard. One must travel over mountains and across dry deserts through lands that are not friendly to the great king Moctezuma and his friends.''

Cortes was adamant; he knew when he was being given the runaround. He had done it often enough himself. He locked eyes with Tuedilli. Forcing him to look down, he demanded that his request to visit Moctezuma be sent to him immediately. Tuedilli agreed to do as he said and left him in a hurry. The meeting was not a total loss. Cortes did acquire one piece of useful information. There were tribes that were not subject to the Aztecs, but were instead their enemies. This might be to his advantage. Caesar had said it long before: *divide and conquer*!

During the time they waited for Moctezuma's response, the Spaniards noticed that on several occasions men stood watch-

ing them from a nearby hilltop, making no effort to come
down as had the other villagers. When they questioned the
Aztec nobles left with them by Tuedilli, they replied only that
they were simple farmers come to take a look at the gods. This
didn't satisfy Cortes, and so he called for Casca to take four
men and go to the watchers on the hill. Casca chose not to
ride, as he thought the horses probably would scare them
away. Instead he took with him Juan and three others who
had shown some small signs of common sense. They walked
up to them slowly, hands extended, smiling to show the
watchers that they were in no danger. They came willingly
enough into the Spanish camp, although Casca could see that
they looked about carefully as if uneasy about something.

These Indians were far different from the Aztecs. They were
bigger men, more heavily muscled, and by Spanish standards,
unbelievably ugly. The cartilage of their noses was so widely
spread and pierced with so many heavy ornaments of crude
gold and rough turquoise that it hung nearly to their mouths.
Their lower lips were pierced by heavy rings of gold set with
colored stones of green and the ever present turquoise. Heavy
rings and plugs pulled their lips down so far that their gums
and lower teeth were exposed. All this they did to make themselves more attractive, but the Spaniards swore that they must
be married to a nation of blind women.

Many of the Aztecs decorated themselves in much the same
fashion, with large earrings and lip plugs, but not to such extremes. Conversing with the Spaniards through Marina, they
said that they were from a city called Cempola, a day's march
distant. The border of their nation was about half that distance, separated from the borders of the Aztecs by a river.
Their Cacique had sent them to find out if the ones who had
come on the floating *teocalli*, or temples, were men or gods.
Cortes was friendly to them as was his habit when first en-
countering new tribes. Giving them small gifts of no value, he
showed them his arms and horses, which had their usual effect
on the savages.

Doña Marina, as she was now being called by the Spanish
soldiery, was asked why the Indians didn't speak to any of
those who were already there. Marina said that they were from
a different tribe. Although much of their language was similar
to that of the Aztecs, they had no love for them. They obeyed

a lord who had managed to keep some of his independence from the Aztecs by the strength of his warriors, though he still had to pay unwilling tribute to the stronger nation. This pleased Cortes mightily, for now he saw that he had the opportunity to acquire allies who would increase his strength greatly in the event of war.

The ambassadors hadn't stopped until they reached the great city of Mexico, all of them near death from exhaustion. When Moctezuma heard their report, an even greater feeling of desperation and fear came over him, especially when he heard about the cannon. Tez-cuzcli fell low to his knees as he made his report:

"Oh, my lord, a thing like a ball of stone burst out of its entrails, throwing sparks and raining fire. The smoke it gives off is most vile in odor, a pestilential smell like that of decayed mud. This smoke penetrates to the brain, causing great feelings of discomfort. If the cannon is aimed at a mountain, the mountain splits open, the very rocks shatter. If it is aimed at a tree, the tree erupts, bursting into thousands of splinters as if it had exploded from the inside."

Moctezuma felt his mind reel, yet he motioned for Tez-cuzcli to continue.

"Their trappings and weapons are all of white iron. They wear iron on their bodies as we do the cotton our women weave. Their bows and their swords are also of iron, as are their helmets and shields. They have strange animals that appear much like huge hornless deer. These deer carry them on their backs faster than the swiftest of our runners and can travel great distances without rest.

"The strangers' bodies are completely covered, leaving only their faces to view. Their skin is white, as if covered with chalk. And their food is much like human food. It is white and not heavy. It is something like straw but with the taste of a cornstalk. It is a little sweet as if flavored with honey. Yes, it tastes of honey and is sweet food.

"Their dogs are monstrous, with flat ears and long, dangling tongues. Their eyes are a burning yellow that flash fire. Their bellies are hollow and their flanks long and narrow. They are tireless and very strong, finding and killing game for the strangers and returning with it in their mouths. They lay the kill before their masters, never eating it themselves unless their masters say it is permissible. Thus do they serve the strangers.''

When they finished their report, Moctezuma felt his heart shrivel with dread. The strangers must be kept away. Fast runners were sent to Tuedilli with his orders that the strangers must not come to Mexico.

Tuedilli returned to speak with Cortes after ten days had passed since their last meeting, and then only after receiving his orders from Mexico. He brought gifts of food and cloth to the Spaniards but told Cortes that the journey to Mexico was very dangerous and long. His king would not grant him permission to escort the Spaniards there, as it might cause them harm to travel over such desolate lands and through hostile regions where tribes lived that were not friends of the Spaniards.

Cortes continued to argue for an immediate reception by the Aztec king, but to no avail. That night all the servants given them by Tuedilli disappeared with the dawn. Every hut was empty. The departing servants had gone back into the brush with the supplies.

Taking four hundred men with him, Cortes headed into the countryside, looking for the natives. After entering the town used as a headquarters by Tuedilli, he found that it was also abandoned. The people had gone, leaving only a sacrificial altar strewn with pieces of paper dipped in blood to show that since last night sacrifices had been made. He turned back to his ships and decided that without the supplies guaranteed him by Tuedilli, he would have to move his base of operations and set sail.

After his talks with the Indians of Cempola, he gave the order to sail toward their lands, where he hoped to secure provisions and allies.

Before they left, Cortes called a meeting of his company. After they had gathered, he solemnly declared: "I claim all this land in the name of Emperor Don Carlos and Spain." Following his declaration, he immediately established a committee of judges and administrators and had himself proclaimed governor of the new lands—pending official confirmation from the emperor, of course.

After a brief reconnaissance by ship, one of Cortes's men

spotted a fair harbor near the lands of Cempola. From there Cortes took to land again, finding the boundary markers separating the Cempolans from the Aztecs on a river three leagues from their landing site.

Casca was with the lead element as they forded the river and moved upstream. They reached a small village before nightfall. He and the three other horsemen approached twenty Indians they'd spotted on a nearby hill. Riding toward them, they made signs of peace while Casca shouted greetings. The Indians took off as if devils were coming after them. They thought, as many others had, that the Spaniards and their horses were one beast. Casca kicked his horse in the flanks and overtook the Indians on a flat piece of ground on the other side of the hill. The Indians had no arms and threw themselves face down to the earth, crying out for mercy. Casca spoke to them softly, using his still-weak vocabulary to allay the worst of their fears. The Indians were brought back to Cortes, who was pleased that they were of the same type as those he had met earlier. Their noses and ears were pierced and stretched to grotesque lengths.

He spoke to them kindly through Marina, saying that he was their friend and wished to speak to their lord and bring him the friendship of another great king. The Indians said that it was too late for him to reach Cempola before nightfall but that they would guide him to a village large enough to feed his men and then take him to Cempola in the morning.

When they neared the village, several of the Indians requested that they be permitted to go in advance of the Spaniards to inform their lord of what had happened and what had been said. They promised they would return in the morning and left their comrades with the Spaniards to serve them until their return. Food was sent from the village as the Spaniards made camp outside to await the morning.

As they had promised, those Cortes had freed to go to Cempola returned with several hundred slaves bearing gifts and food. They bowed low to Cortes, dipping straws in their blood to honor him; then they gave him their master's words. The strangers would be welcome. They told Cortes privately that their lord was a very large man, and to travel any distance was too difficult for him, as he weighed as much as three or four average men.

Leading them onto a good road, they soon reached Cempola, which was only a few miles farther on. They passed through orchards and fields and were greeted by the Indians with flowers and gifts. Six horsemen had ridden ahead into the city and returned to Cortes with the words that the courtyards of Cempola were covered in silver plate. Cortes sent them back with orders to show no surprise at anything they might see. The Indians must never think they had anything which was better than what the Castilians were used to.

CHAPTER TEN

They entered the streets of Cempola on a wide tree-lined avenue filled with awed natives, gaping in wonder at the sight of the Spaniards on their horses. The ranks were fully armored and were being led into the city by Cortes. In the center of the column, the cannon were being guarded by the best of the infantry. They came to a wide square with high walls and battlements. To the embarrassment of those who had reported that the walls of Cempola were lined with silver, they found instead that the Cempolans had used a plaster made of polished gypsum that gleamed in the sun as if it were made of the precious metal.

Inside the enclosure were rooms and apartments. At the far side stood seven towers that were separated from each other, each in its turn a bit taller than the next.

The Spaniards waited in silence, eyes watching the walls of the battlements for any sign of treachery. The cannon had been primed before the march and were ready to be fired. Cortes was greeted by nobles of the city who bowed low before him and asked if he would accompany them to their lord's palace only a few steps away. This he did, escorted by several of his officers and Casca. He had decided on the latter as an afterthought.

Tazcamili, the lord of Cempola, came out of his palace to the edge of the steps and halted. On each side of him was a strong, nearly nude warrior holding his arm to give him support. It was true. He was nearly as big as four men, not in size but in girth. The man was a mountain of fat and suet. His eyes were nearly lost in folds of tissue. It was easy to see why he didn't travel very far and had need of the constant attendance of two stout warriors. They would have a hard time of it if he ever slipped and fell. Getting him back to his feet would be a major operation. The lord of Cempola never lay down to sleep. Such was his size that if he did, he would have died from the sheer weight of his own body on his rib cage and heart. He had to sleep in the sitting position or not sleep at all.

Advancing up the stairs, Cortes was all smiles as he held out his hands in greeting. The two men bowed to each other and through Marina and Gerónimo gave greetings, after which Tazcamili retired to the interior of his palace. The Spaniards were shown to large spacious rooms and apartments. Cortes was not going to relax his security despite the friendly reception. His men were distributed throughout the rooms, the cannon were positioned to cover the main entrance, and the horses were put under strict guard. Cortes ordered that no one, on pain of death, was to go outside without his permission. There was always the chance that they were being brought into a trap of some kind.

Food was provided and pallets and hammocks brought for their use. Cortes and Tazcamili would meet again on the morrow. The lord of Cempola claimed that pressing duties were keeping him from paying his respects properly as he wished to do on this fortunate day.

Cortes had noticed Casca's recently acquired grasp of the tongue of the natives and thought it prudent to have him by his side when they met with Tazcamili. One could never tell when the savages might be plotting, and if they thought no Spaniard spoke their barbarous language, they might reveal information that could prove to be of value to the Spaniard. Casca was not to speak Nahual to the Indians. He was instructed to listen only and report if he heard anything of interest.

The next day, after the exchanging of a few small gifts, the two leaders got down to business. With his escort of fifty officers, Cortes went to the palace of Tazcamili. The rest were to obey his orders as stated earlier.

Taking Cortes and his officers with him into a low room thatched with palm fronds, Tazcamili offered them seats on short benches carved from one piece of wood like chipping blocks. Marina sat by Cortes, her eyes never leaving those of Tazcamili. She listened and faithfully rendered the lord's words to her master as best she could. Casca said nothing; he merely found a spot near one of Tazcamili's nobles and sat with them, watching those at the table maneuver one another about for the best advantage. Tazcamili was no match for the sophistication of the European. He had the added disadvantage of being in superstitious awe of the men in iron, though he spoke to them as he would have to any other of noble birth.

Cortes sweet-talked Tazcamili, telling him, in the name of his king, Don Carlos, about his mission to bring good things to the people he met. Tazcamili listened carefully, noting in the telling that Cortes did not speak overly well of the Aztecs and their treatment of him. Although he said nothing ill of them, much could be discerned by what was not spoken.

Tazcamili in turn said to the Spaniard, "Noble lord, I think that it would be a good thing if you know something of my people, for their tale is the same as most of those of these lands. Once we were our own masters; that was before the Mexicas came out of the deserts. Before the Aztecs settled in the valley and built their city of Tenochtitlán, they sent their priests to work evil among the peaceful tribes, searching out their weaknesses and then subjugating them. If a nation became the willing vassal of the Aztecs, it was made certain they would never rise against them in strength. To accomplish this, these vassals were required to send levees of young men and women to the Aztec altars.

"If a nation fights them and is defeated, their warriors are taken to be sacrificed to the Aztec war gods. Those who resisted Moctezuma would have their flesh fed to his warriors after the sacrifice. And those who survived would be forced to work from the rising of the sun to its setting, even the women and children. If the harvests were poor, they were left to starve, with no compassion or pity shown to any. On all tribes, vassal or conquered, they inflict heavy taxes and tribute, giving nothing in return other than the priest's dagger. If any complain, they are slain. The Aztecs were never known for compassion in their treatment of those they considered beneath them.''

Tazcamili paused to catch his breath as he tried to read the face of his guest. Seeing that Cortes was showing obvious sympathy to his words and shock over the manner in which the subjects of Moctezuma were treated, he continued with renewed strength, for he had heard how the few men of the Spaniards had defeated the warriors of Tabasco. He told Cortes of Tenochtitlán, the great city built on the waters of the lake Texcoco. He told him of the wealth, power, and splendor of the Aztec empire, noting the gleam in Cortes's eye when he spoke of the gold paid as tribute to the king of Mexica. Then he spoke of the other tribes.

"My lord, I think it is fitting that you should know that not all tribes are completely dominated by the Aztecs, even if they do pay tribute. There are still many who carry their heads high with pride and courage and cling to their gods. The Tlaxcalans, Totonacs, Huejotzingo, and many others are enemies of Moctezuma, and after what has happened at Tabasco, I am sure they would be more than ready to make an alliance with the men of iron, if it was so desired.''

Cortes didn't wish to commit himself to an alliance this soon; it would be premature. But he was more than pleased at the idea of having thousands of Indian allies to do his bidding if needed. He spoke gently to Tazcamili. "My good lord, I am most grieved at what you have said concerning the treatment of your people and others by the Aztecs. Rest assured that when I speak to Moctezuma, I shall use all that is in my power to make him see that justice is given. For that is the manner in which things are done in my country by my lord and master, Don Carlos, king of Spain, who is now your good friend. As you have offered your friendship to me, so it is in turn given to my master, and his power to protect you is now an obligation that I gladly assume in his name.''

Cortes left, remarking that he had been gone too long from his ships and that it was time for him to return and see to the needs of his men. Tazcamili smiled through blubbery lips as he offered Cortes the honor of being a guest in his city, where he would provide all that his new friend's men might need.

However, if Cortes wished to return to his ships, it was only a short distance and they could continue their discussions at a later date. Before Cortes departed, Tazcamili called to his chamberlain and had gifts brought in for the Spaniard. Eight Indian girls, one of whom was his own niece, were given as wives for the officers of Cortes's company. Though the women were not very attractive by his standards, Cortes knew that to refuse them would be a deadly insult. He accepted the gift of the women and took his leave. The women were carried on litters to their rooms, where he distributed them among his officers, of whom Casca was not one, and for that Casca was, to say the least, very thankful.

When they left Cempola, it took only a day's march to reach a city on the river called Quiahuixtlan, a city of the Totonacs. His ships had not arrived there yet, and so he made himself at home at the invitation of the town chief, who already had been informed of his coming by Tazcamili. Here, Cortes received more proof that not all the towns and nations of this land were under the complete control of Moctezuma.

Escorted into the city by the elders of the town, they were taken to the city square, where balls of copal, a resinous incense, were burned in a clay brazier. The smoke was waved with fans over Cortes and his men as a kind of ceremony they observed with their lords and their gods.

The chief of the town repeated almost the exact sentiments of Tazcamili, stating in detail that Moctezuma would be very angry at his receiving the Spaniard, for they had been given orders that none were to aid the strangers or give them comfort of any kind.

As they were speaking, Casca looked out the door and saw a group of eighteen men crossing the square. He knew a bureaucrat when he saw one. Each man carried a thick short wand and a feathered flyflap purse. The Totonacs became extremely agitated, whispering to Cortes that they were there to collect tribute for Moctezuma. They were very much afraid that the tax men would report back that Cortes and his men had been given comfort and shelter. For that, Moctezuma was quite capable of having every man, woman, and child in the village put to death. Keeping one hand on his sword and one eye on the Aztecs, Casca heard Cortes as he rose from his bench and told the Totonacs; "I promise you this: The lord Moctezuma

will not harm you for giving me shelter. He will reward you
for your kindness. But if he does not, I promise you, as I did
the lord of Cempola, that I will protect the friends of Spain
against all who would do them harm. My soldiers are the equal
of a thousand Aztecs, as you have witnessed by the battle of
Tabasco. Moctezuma also knows my power and will not have
me for a foe.''

The Totonac chief had started to rise to his feet to bow
before the Aztecs, when Cortes stopped him. Having decided
to play his hand a bit further, he told the chief and his elders:
''To show you what I and my men can do, order your men to
seize these tax collectors of Moctezuma, for I shall be with
you, and not even the great Moctezuma himself will be able to
molest you. Such is his respect for me.''

Casca thought that Cortes might have let his mouth overload his ass, but the Totonacs did as he said. They grabbed the
Aztecs, and when they resisted, they had them whipped. Then
they tied their hands and feet to a long pole and held the pole
as if the Aztecs were suckling pigs before the roast. Once they
made the move, the Totonacs wanted to go all the way and kill
the tax men to prevent them from returning to tell of their
treatment. But Cortes persuaded them not to do so for the
time being. At Cortes's insistence, the tax men were placed in
a room adjoining those of the Spaniards. A fire was built, and
Cortes posted guards at the door. After completing this small
task, he left for his rooms to rest; he had things yet to do this
evening.

Waiting till he was sure the Indians were asleep, Cortes went
to Gerónimo de Aquilar and told him to release two of the
Aztecs and bring them to his rooms. This was done as ordered,
and when the Aztecs were brought before Cortes, he professed
no knowledge of how they had been captured while in the process of performing their duty of collecting lawful tribute for
their master, Moctezuma.

The tax men begged Cortes to protect them, for the men of
the Totonacs were known to have no love for the Mexicas.

Cortes smiled behind his beard before answering them. ''I
should indeed be sorry if the servants of the lord Moctezuma
became injured or distressed in my presence. But I will look
after you and see that you are brought to safety. You should
thank God and myself for your freedom—God because he has

brought me to your lands, me because I wish to be no more than a good friend to your king. Therefore, you will take this message back with you to Moctezuma. Tell his majesty that I consider him my friend and desire to serve him as such. I know of his fame, power, and goodness. Tell him also that I am pleased that chance gave me the opportunity to demonstrate my affection for him by arranging the release of your own persons from the hostile hands of the Totonacs.

"You will also say that it is possible that I will grow weary of his refusing my hand in friendship, as I have already demonstrated to Tuedilli. Let his majesty arrange with all haste our inevitable meeting and take the steps necessary to see that all obstacles are removed from our paths that we may meet as brothers. If this is not done, then the responsibility for the future lies with him, not me."

After the tax men were given food and water, they were set free at the edge of town. Cortes had promised them that he would take charge of those left behind and keep them safe until he heard from Moctezuma or his representative.

The Mexicas were more than happy to swear to do as he had bidden them and quickly disappeared, putting as many leagues between themselves and the Totonacs as possible, each of them swearing to speak to his supervisor about a transfer to a less hostile territory.

In the morning, Tazcamili was furious with the escape of the two prisoners but didn't have the nerve to question the Spaniard about it. He blamed it on traitors among his own people who somehow had managed to spirit them out of his city. Now the Aztecs were sure to come and so they might as well put the rest of the Mexicas to death and have some fun before they themselves were taken to the altars of Huitzilopochtli.

Casca had to admire the shrewdness of Cortes, who now offered to take full responsibility for the remaining prisoners if Tazcamili would give them to him. Furthermore, he promised the Totonacs the full support of the Spanish arms if the Aztecs sought reprisals.

Tazcamili agreed, turning the rest of the tax men over to Cortes, who had them taken out to his ships for safekeeping.

The people of Cempola and Quiahuixtlan, along with their chieftains, cried out for Cortes to become their leader and honor his promise of full support in the event of war with the Aztecs. They would no longer serve the Mexicas but would offer themselves and their lands as willing vassals to the king of Spain.

This was too good an opportunity to pass up. It had gone better than Cortes had imagined. In one stroke he had two tribes at his feet.

Before accepting, however, he spoke to them. "Think carefully about what you are doing. Moctezuma is a very powerful king, but if you so desire and swear to be faithful to me, then I will accept command of your tribes and protect you even though the entire army of the Aztecs comes forth. They cannot stand against the valor of Spain and the true God, who is now your sovereign lord as he is mine."

When he asked how many warriors they could muster between them, he was astounded when they said that they could field a hundred thousand men if all the cities and villages rallied to them. One hundred thousand warriors, and the Aztecs ruled over them as if they were dogs. Well, with enough dogs, who knew? He ordered them to send runners to all the cities they knew of that were of a like mind and wished to throw off the yoke of Aztec oppression and join with the forces of Cortes to bring a new day to this land and its peoples.

Throughout the region spread the word of the demigods who had offered them protection. Before ten days had passed, there was not a single Aztec tax collector or official left. They either had left or had been taken captive. In several cases, they had been killed and eaten.

Casca had to admire the deftness with which Cortes made himself indispensable to the rebellious tribes. They didn't trust each other, and none would give command to any who was not of their tribe; therefore, they could never unite with enough strength to overthrow the Aztecs. But Cortes was another matter. He didn't belong to any tribe; therefore, he was acceptable to all as a leader. Also, most believed that the Spaniards had supernatural powers of some sort.

While waiting for the next turn of events, Cortes marked out a permanent site near his ships, bringing a thousand workers in from Cempola and neighboring tribes to aid him in the founding of his new city, to which he gave the name of Villa Rica de la Vera Cruz, or Rich City of the True Cross.

As construction of permanent buildings was in progress, two nephews of Moctezuma, richly dressed in fine mantles and wearing armbands of beaten gold and necklaces of silver set with rubies and emeralds, presented themselves. They were accompanied by four wise elders who acted as advisers. They offered Cortes gifts of cotton mantles and a helmet full of gold grains valued at two thousand castellanos. They said, "Our lord Moctezuma has sent to you this token as you requested. He is hoping that it might help to cure the sickness you spoke of and asked that it also be accepted as a token of his appreciation for your saving the lives of two of his servants and preventing the others in his service from being killed by the barbarians.

"Our master further wishes us to assure you of his high regard and affection. He asks that you release the others who are held on board your ships." The ambassadors went to extremes to make certain that Cortes understood that Moctezuma held him in no way responsible for the evil done by the Cempolans and their allies. As for when Cortes might expect to meet their master, they could not yet give a time. At the moment, their lord was occupied with matters of state, and several small wars on his borders had to be attended to. But Cortes was to rest assured that all would be as he wished if he was patient.

Cortes, however, had no intention of being patient. He had things moving the way he wanted them and needed to keep the pressure on to see that they continued in his favor. He gave the nephews of Moctezuma some small gifts of glass, iron, and clothing and then told them that they would have to return to Tenochtitlán when they had rested for a day and night.

During this time, Casca and Marina spent many more hours together. With the arrival of the kinsmen of Moctezuma, he had the feeling that time was running short and that there was much he still needed to know. Several times he thought he saw a strange look in Marina's eyes as they talked. She'd look at him wonderingly and then turn her gaze elsewhere. Juan noticed the looks she gave his friend but simply put it down to feminine curiosity about Casca's merits as a lover. As to his learning their barbaric tongue, he thought it much more practical for the savages to learn Spanish. When he told Casca of his thinking concerning Marina, Casca merely looked at him as if he were a bit simple-minded. Marina had never even touched him, not once had she even laid a hand on him, even in the most casual manner. If there was anything to wonder about, perhaps it was that.

The night before the ambassadors were to leave, Casca lay on his bunk in the small adobe room he shared with Juan. Tonight his small friend was on guard duty. The heaviness of the night had made him remove his shirt so that he could sleep. He used a thin Indian blanket for a coverlet. When he turned in his sleep, the blanket slipped down to his waist. A glow from the moon outside the single window brought a glow to the scars on his chest and arms. A shadow moved aside the ragged blanket serving as a door to his bare quarters. Marina stood three feet away from the sleeping soldier, her eyes taking in every mark on the muscled body. She shivered, but not with the chill of the evening, for there was none. With trembling fingers, she undid the single knot at her shoulder, letting her dress fall to the bare earth of the hut's floor. Moving a bit closer to the sleeping man, she resisted the compulsion to touch the scar running from his eye to the corner of his mouth. She removed the tortoiseshell comb which held up her thick hair, letting it fall to the small of her back in thick, dark waves. She passed in front of the light of the moon, her shadow moving across Casca's closed eyes.

His eyes jerked open as the shadow passed over them, his hand reaching for the knife by his side. The touch of a warm, soft hand kept him from striking. Marina moved the cover away from him, laying her body close to his. She still shivered from head to toe. She gave herself to the scar-faced man that night, never speaking a word until an hour before dawn, when she rose to dress. For Casca it had been a strange experience. He was certainly no stranger to women, but this had been something different. The manner of her treatment and love-making had a texture to it that he couldn't find words to express. She was putting the tortoiseshell comb back into her hair when he asked, "Why?"

Marina smiled down at him. "Do you have to ask?"

Casca nodded his head in the affirmative. Marina sat back down on the side of his cot. "I have made an offering to you, and you have accepted it. Therefore, I am blessed. I know who you are, for I have been to Tenochtitlán, and the old city of the gods, where I have seen your face on the mask of the god. You are he who was foretold, and I am the first to make a sacrifice to you. Therefore, I am blessed among women.''

Marina rose to leave, stopping at the blanket covering the door. She made one more statement. ''I was not completely certain until I saw your body and the mark of the sacrificial dagger upon it. You are the god! There could be no one else. As to why you choose to let Cortes act as the leader, that is your business and not mine to question. I leave you now, Tectli Quetza.'' She was half out the door before he heard her whisper, with a tiny laugh so soft that he wasn't certain he heard her correctly, ''If you ever feel the need for another offering, do not hesitate to call.''

CHAPTER ELEVEN

Casca watched the departing backs of the nephews of Moctezuma. The events of the last weeks were giving him an uneasy
feeling that Cortes was going to rip the country apart and in
the process its people too. He knew that the Aztecs were barbarous in their customs, even to the eating of human flesh, but
other cultures had gone through the same evolutionary process. The question in his mind concerned what to do. He had
no real desire for the gold of Moctezuma or for power. He
knew full well that both of those things would be temporary at
best.

For a time this land had been home to him, and he had liked
the people. They had a greatness to them that if allowed to
grow could make them one of the great peoples of the world.
But should they be allowed to grow if in the process they put
thousands upon thousands of more innocent people on their
altars?

The Spaniards were not a great deal better; witness their Inquisition and the cheerful slaughtering of anyone who wasn't
a Catholic. But the Spaniards would, if history was any gauge,
grow out of their insanity faster than the isolated cultures of
the Indians.

Impulse had directed his feet more than once over the cen-

turies. He left his horse behind, telling the stablers to take care
of him; he was going to scout around a bit. As he left the
camp, a hail stopped his steps. Juan was running up to him.
"Where are you going?"

Casca didn't feel like going into the story of his life, and so
he just told him, "I have something to do that can't be
stopped. You stay here until I get back. If you go on the march
before I return, take my horse."

Juan knew that there was nothing he could do to change his
compadre's mind. He only asked, "Does this have something
to do with your learning their tongue?"

Casca nodded. "That and other things I don't have time to
tell you of. So just go back and let me do that which I have
to." He left Juan standing on the trail as he double-timed it
after the nephews of Moctezuma. Juan watched the broad
back disappear where the trail curved by a grove of tall maguey plants. He wondered if he'd ever see Casca again. He just
didn't understand.

It took him only a few minutes to catch up to the ambassador's party, where they had rejoined their escort of two thousand warriors from the Coyote Clan. The members of the clan
were brilliantly costumed men armed with *macamas*, spears,
and bows, their faces painted with black and red bands. On
their heads were headdresses of bright feathers, and on their
shields the likeness of the coyote. When the ambassadors had
neared the camp of the Spaniards, they had ordered the escort
to remain behind so that they would not make a threatening
image to the gods from the sea. Now they waited to return the
nephews of the king back to him, acting as a bodyguard for
them through the now not so secure lands between them and
Tenochtitlán.

He hailed them as soon as he was out of sight and earshot of
the Spanish camp.

It was with some surprise that Xocomilco and Tletzin found
one of the strangers speaking to them in their tongue and
demanding to be taken to Tenochtitlán to see the king. This
presented them with a problem. Their orders were to keep the
Spaniards away from Tenochtitlán. Now this lone scar-faced
stranger wished to go with them. The elders conferred among
themselves before arriving at a decision. The man would have
to stay behind. Moctezuma had made it clear that he did not

wish to have the Spaniards in his city.

That would have been it, except that Casca had made up his mind that he was going to go whether they liked it or not. When they left, he followed behind, keeping their pace. They marched all that day until nightfall, when the ambassadors and their escort took shelter in a village where food and beds were provided for them. Again they held conference over what to do about the man on their trail. They could not just let him follow them all the way home. He had to be stopped. But how?

Maxtcli, a captain of the Coyotes and a noble warrior with the emblems of honor on his shield and a tunic for taking many prisoners, decided to end the wise men's arguments through direct action. He had watched the Spaniard and saw nothing different about him other than the pale, reddish color of his skin and his light hair. He ate as did other men and relieved his body of its wastes as did normal men. Then why all this talk from the elders about what to do? He would stop this intruder from following them and do so in a manner that all would notice and bear witness to. Perhaps that would put a stop to the fears about these ugly, pale men being gods.

He had prepared himself, painting his face with red and black stripes from eyes to ears and mouth to jawbone. He dressed carefully in a jacket of padded cotton over which he wore a tunic of green parrot feathers. Holding his hide shield with the four nose moons on it and the *macama* lined with razor-sharp pieces of obsidian, he was ready to prove the humanity of the so-called god from the sea.

His preparations did not go unnoticed by the elders and their charges. One started to voice his protest at what the warrior obviously had in mind, but then he realized that here was a possible solution to their problem. Maxtcli was acting on his own without their knowledge or consent. If he killed the stranger, Moctezuma's anger would not be at them, for they had nothing to do with it. If the stranger killed the warrior, they would still be innocent of wrongdoing, for Maxtcli would have brought it on himself.

Taking his apprentice with him to carry his extra weapons, Maxtcli went to where the stranger had made his small camp outside the village. His passage attracted the attention of others of his clan, and they silently followed him. They knew from the look on his face and his paint that someone was going to die. Maxtcli was a handsome man, proud of his strength and race, strong and fearless in battle. Now he was going to challenge one who was said to be a god or at least a demigod.

Maxtcli said nothing as he strode proudly forward, the feathers of his battle dress waving proudly. By the time he reached the campfire of the stranger, there was a full audience ready for the show, including many of the villagers and the nephews of Moctezuma, who chose to stay in the background and out of sight.

The tread of many feet brought Casca's head around. He was going to have company. Resigned to what he knew was coming, he rose to his feet, standing in the glow of the fire, where a hare was roasting on a spit. With regret he knew that it was more than likely that he was not going to be able to have it for his supper.

Maxtcli walked straight up to Casca, standing face to face with him, his eyes steady on the pale one's.

"Go back or die."

Casca knew from the look on the warrior's face that he was not going to listen to any other suggestions. His mind was locked up.

The crowd moved around them, forming a loose circle of seminaked painted and feathered bodies. In the glow of the campfire they could have been mistaken for some kind of strange exotic birds of prey, hesitant, expectant, waiting. Casca nodded his head in acceptance of the inevitable. Stepping back a pace, he drew his sword, regretting that he had taken off his breastplate while waiting to eat. He knew the effect that the razor-edged piece of obsidian had on human flesh.

Twisting his tongue around the still uncomfortable words, he spoke to his opponent. "I am sorry that this has come to pass. Have you prepared yourself to meet your gods?"

Maxtcli expanded his chest. Raising the *macama* above his head, he laughed. "I have no need of that. An Aztec is always ready to meet his destiny, for we are the children of Huitzilopochtli. To him I have sworn to offer a sacrifice this night."

Casca had no desire to kill the man, but this was not the first time pride and vanity had brought a man his death; it would

not be the last. Maxtcli started to move forward but was
stopped as Casca raised his hand. "Not yet." Removing his
tunic, he stood bare-chested and armed. In the glow of the
fire, the red embers turned his scars into streaks of quivering
blood marks.

For the first time Maxtcli looked a bit uneasy. He couldn't
remove his eyes from the scars that crisscrossed Casca's chest
and body. Deep trenches ran along the stranger's arms, and
the deep ragged-edged scar in the center of the chest leaped out
at him. The beginnings of doubt set into his mind. This man
should have been dead a dozen times over.

Casca loosened his arms and chest. Sucking in air, he
flexed, knowing the impression his mangled body was having
on the superstitious Indians. He still hoped he would be able
to avoid the fight. As the muscles under his skin moved, the
scars rippled like serpents with a life of their own. They
twisted and turned under his skin.

Casca spoke once more. "You are a brave man, but this
fight does not have to be, for you cannot win. See the marks
on my body! How can you offer the burning flower to the
gods when I have already been under the knife of the priests?"

His voice rose in strength, the words coming easier.

"Has a man such as I ever been to your lands in your
lifetime? No! Yet I know of the great city of Teotihuacan and
the temples of the sun and moon. I know Tlaloc who brings
the rains. It is his image which lies beside the symbol of the
Serpent God on the stairs leading to the place of sacrifice. I
know of the death masks of the kings and where they lie in the
temple of the serpent. All this I know and have seen long
before your father's father drew his first breath. I walked this
land when your nation and people did not exist. Do not bring
death upon yourself, for I have no desire to spill your blood.
Leave your death to another and take me to Moctezuma."

Maxtcli's heart pounded in his chest. He was now truly
frightened of what he had seen and heard. The stranger knew
things that no one like him could have known. Was it possible? Maxtcli pushed the fear back, thinking, No! He is trying
to trick me. Someone has told him of these things. He is only a
man, no more, and as such, he will die.

Maxtcli whipped his courage into a flame and cried out to
the gods as he swung the heavy *macama*, aiming for the head

of the foreigner. Casca blocked it with ease and countered with a side stroke, opening up Maxtcli's face to the bone. Maxtcli came again, his hide shield covering him as he moved in to the attack. Casca's steel blade cut the shield to ribbons. Then he hacked the wooden haft of the *macama* to splinters. Neither the Aztec warrior nor his weapons were even close to being a match for the skills of one who had fought in the Circus Maximus and had been trained in the School of Gladiators under the tutelage of Corvu the Lanista. For Casca it was nearly like fighting one of the *andabate*, the condemned men who were blinded and then put into the arena to fight with knives. Still he tried to avoid killing the man, using his blade only to prick and tease, trying to wear Maxtcli down to where he wouldn't have to take his life.

It was too late for such thoughts. Maxtcli had been humiliated. He was bleeding from a dozen cuts, and his shield and weapon had been destroyed as if they were children's toys. And this pale ugly thing before him bobbed and weaved, teasing and toying with him. He would not be humiliated. He was a war captain who had been honored by Moctezuma himself and given his emblems of courage by the king's own hand. If he could not kill this thing before him, he would at least make sure that his own death song would be sung with honor throughout the lands of the Mexicas. He lunged at Casca, not trying to avoid the sword. He threw one arm around Casca's shoulder as the other hand grasped Casca's sword wrist.

The movement was a surprise. It caught Casca off guard. The weight of Maxtcli's body pressed him back a step. Then Maxtcli quit his forward pressure and stepped a full pace back to his rear. Before Casca could react, Maxtcli moved forward again. This time he jerked Casca's sword wrist up and over their center. Ramming his body on the point, he pushed hard. He clawed at Casca's shoulders as he pulled himself onto the steel of Castile. His mouth filled with blood as his lungs were ripped apart. Throwing his head back, neck muscles extended, mouth pouring out bright scarlet blood, he cried out to Huitzilopochtli to take his offering. He jerked his body to the side and twisted so that the sword slid sideways from his lungs to sever the great muscle of his heart. He had made his sacrifice to his god as he had sworn to do.

The manner in which Maxtcli died and the futility of his

effort to kill Casca silenced the watchers, many of whom touched hidden totems to ward off evil. Casca walked slowly over to the nephews, Xocomilco and Tletzin. The sweat gleamed on his torso as he held his blood-dripping sword in his hand. The scar running along the side of his face seemed much paler than before. Pointing the blade at them, his voice dull and deadly, he said, "Now will you lead me to Tenochtitlán, or do others have to die this night? I am weary of your refusals. Do not try my patience further, for you are dealing with things you know nothing of. Only the lord Moctezuma can judge what I have to say and in turn be judged."

Xocomilco was not a brave man by nature. He was trained not as a warrior but as a politician. This man or thing before him was primal violence, and he knew that the wrong word would mean his death. The warriors of his escort didn't give him much comfort, and he wasn't certain that they could have done any good. Perhaps this man had been speaking the truth about knowing things long past and having walked in the city of the gods. Those questions, augmented by superstitious fear, were too much for him to deal with. He knelt down before the scarred man.

"Lord, I must obey my king or give up my life. He has commanded that no one give any of your people any assistance or aid in reaching our capital. There is nothing I can do to help you, though you take my life. However, I have not received any instructions to do you harm. This act against you this night was not of our doing. It was completely the idea of Maxtcli, who has now sent his spirit to the gods of our fathers. If you choose to follow after us, there would be nothing I could do to hinder you."

Casca accepted that. He understood the man's fear for his life. He knew that even though he didn't give aid to Casca, he still might be killed for not doing something to prevent his following after them. But that was his problem. Casca had more important things to consider than the lives of one or two or even a hundred men. It had long since been proved that human life was a very cheap commodity where the future of nations was concerned, and the individual became immediately expendable to the so-called greater good.

Lowering his sword point, he motioned for Xocomilco to rise and said, "I agree. You may go on ahead of me, and I shall follow. But know this. At the first sign of treachery, I shall come for you and kill you in a manner that will give your children nightmares for the rest of their lives."

The Aztecs left the campfire, taking the body of Maxtcli with them. They returned to their beds shaken at what they had seen this night. If the scar-faced man was representative of what all the Spaniards were like, they were truly a most fearsome people and not completely human.

CHAPTER TWELVE

In the morning, the ambassadors and their escort took to the trail again. Casca was ready. He put his armor in his pack and followed after them. He could have reached Tenochtitlán on his own, but it was best this way. If he hadn't agreed with the Aztec ambassadors, he would have had to fight every step of the way. Now, if he was lucky, he would not have to exert himself much more and still would reach his objective.

He trailed after them as they passed through the heavy, tropical forests and began the slow climb to the mountains, where the air grew thin and the lungs labored. He began to see landmarks that were familiar as they neared the passes that led to the high desert. He knew that across them lay the great lakes where the city of Tenochtitlán awaited his arrival in the valley of Mexico.

If he wanted food, he took it from the cooking pots of the villages they passed through, not caring whether it was dog meat or even the large lizards the Indians were so fond of. There were no protests, only looks of wonder at his paleness. If he touched an object, it was carefully wrapped and given to a priest, for it was well known that magic could be made through the use of objects that had been touched or drunk from by a god.

In each of the villages, the story of his contest with Maxtcli was repeated with wonder. In the telling the story grew greater, for Maxtcli had been a great and famous warrior.

Casca was left alone. If he came near a child, the mother or father would scoop it up out of his path and cover its eyes so that it would not have its soul stolen by the gods, for that is what the people of the tribes were beginning to call all the Spaniards. The story told of the scarred one proved that at the very least they had powers beyond those of mere mortals.

Casca had learned to use his wounds to his advantage. The sight of those scars on his body brought instant fear to the Indians. Wounds were something they understood, and those on the body of the god ensured that he would not be bothered by any on his journey. When he began the trek across the desert, he could see a smoking mountain in the distance and knew that he was nearing the end of his journey.

The mountain had been sacred long before the Aztecs had settled in the green valley of the lakes. It was called Popocatepetl, the smoking mountain, and not far away was its sister mountain, Ixtaccihuatl, or the white woman, named for the pale ash and snow that rested on its crater's rim. These ancient volcanoes had witnessed the rise and fall of many peoples including those Casca, as the Quetza, had ruled over—the Teotec, who now were only distant memories in the minds of the Aztecs as the builders of the city of the gods, Teotihuacan.

He passed through many small towns with populations numbering only a thousand and several large cities, the most important of which was Cholula, a holy center where the principal god to whom they made sacrifice was the Quetza.

On the borders of the valley of Mexico were other cities with populations of over fifty thousand. The people here did not have the look of the Aztec about them. Subject or vassal, in the faces of most he saw no love for the brilliantly clad warriors who treated them with contempt and disdain.

The capital city of the Aztecs could be reached only after crossing the deserts and then descending into the broad valley. As they came closer, they had to pass large fields of the spiny maguey plant, hills spotted with hundreds of the tall white flowering yucca, and a few patches set aside for maize. Once inside the valley, every bit of arable land was used for cultivation of foodstuffs, mostly maize, the staple of the Aztec diet.

When they left the desert and passed close to the towns built around five lakes, hundreds gathered to watch them, gawking in wonder at the strangers. All the cities were well built, clean, and orderly. Temples and gardens were everywhere, their walls covered with carvings and painted frescoes. The strange art of this land decorated nearly every flat space on both the insides and outsides of buildings and walls.

He passed several cities on the edge of one lake, Tlapan, Tizapan, and Coyohuacan, before they reached Chapultepec, where a broad causeway led to the island city of Tenochtitlán. The escort of Coyote warriors was relieved at the gates of the city by the Eagle Knights of the palace guard. They took over the responsibility for guiding the ambassadors to the palace of Moctezuma.

Casca had his way blocked by fifty fully armed warriors who made their bows, lances, and hand weapons obvious. He got the message that he was not to follow after the nephews of Moctezuma.

Fast runners had gone ahead of the party, and Moctezuma had known of the coming of the stranger for some days before his arrival. He still had no wish to see the man face to face but ordered that he be treated as a guest and shown all courtesy. The only thing to be denied him was access to the king's presence. He would have to wait until he was sent for. Other than that, he could have complete freedom of the other cities but could not enter the walls of Tenochtitlán.

Casca was given reluctant greetings by a priest, a nasty-looking bastard whose long, greasy hair hung nearly to his waist and smelled of blood. The priest indicated that Casca was to leave the causeway and follow him. He led him to a house in Chapultepec and he made it clear that Casca was to live there. It was much like those of the other cities, with a low roof, small windows, and walls painted with bright frescoes depicting Aztec life and their gods. Guards were stationed at every exit including the windows.

The priest's manner made it obvious that he did not like having any intercourse with the stranger. Using as few words as possible, he made it clear that Casca could go where he wished as long as he stayed away from Moctezuma and his city. The guards were there to make certain he was not bothered and to ensure his own protection and security until

Moctezuma decided what he wished to do about him.

Personally, the priest hoped that the scarred one would be given to him as an offering to Huitzilopochtli or even for the mother of the gods, Coatlicue, who, wearing her crown of snake heads and necklace of hearts and chopped-off hands, waited in her temple by the Place of Reeds. Sometimes the priest felt that she was not given her fair share of the blood offerings.

Casca entered the low rooms of his new abode without comment. He was not ready to push the issue of seeing Moctezuma to the breaking point yet. He had done well to get this far. Now he would take the time to learn of the Aztecs and their people. He would see what they were really like and what their future might be. Once this was done, he would see Moctezuma. Of that he had no doubt. When he was ready, the king of the Aztecs would grant him an audience. That was not conjecture; it was destiny.

For now he was content to wander the valley of Mexico, walk in the markets, watch the people, and learn. They had much that was good about them but had more that was not. If a man admired the Spartans, he would love the Aztecs. From birth, they had a rigid system that allowed no deviation. Even the number of corn cakes that one could eat each day was controlled. Maize was the property of the state. Beans and other vegetables or even meat could be owned or bartered for, but maize was the staple, and the staple was controlled.

Children of the Aztecs who became farmers or craftsmen were first trained as priests or warriors. Here even the priests went into battle for the glory of the gods. Many of them achieved great fame for their prowess and courage. Children of the Aztecs were punished by regulated methods dependent on their age. A disobedient child of nine could be punished by being beaten with a rod or else be tied hand and foot and have his body and limbs pricked with the sharp points of the maguey. Girls were treated slightly better. As the children grew older, the punishments grew more harsh.

The Aztecs were extremely moral, demanding a high standard of conduct from everyone. Thievery and drunkenness could be punished by death, as could adultery on the part of a woman. A married man could have relations with a woman only if she was not married. Once wed, fidelity was demanded

of the women and was enforced strictly. Only after they
reached the age of seventy were they permitted to drink to
excess, which most of them did. Because of their age, their
actions were forgiven them; the elderly were honored and
respected.

Throughout their lives, religious doctrine was rigidly enforced with an intolerance that Torquemada would have en-
vied. To Casca's mind, the Aztecs were nearly Catholic in
their attitudes toward heretics and blasphemers.

He went out to visit other cities. Leaving behind his Spanish
dress, he wore the loose mantle of the Indians as well as their
loincloth. He covered his head with a small cloth cap of cotton. If he wasn't looked at too closely, he was ignored, at least
until his escort of Eagle Knights was noted. Everywhere he
went, they accompanied him. All that he did, said, touched,
smelled, or looked at was noted and reported back to Moctezuma.

The cities of the Aztecs were built around five connecting
lakes. To the north was Xaltocan and Zumpango, to the south
Xochimilco and Chalco, and between them the most sacred of
all, where Tenochtitlán rested on its island, was Lake Texcoco. All of these were connected by canals and drawbridges.
On the lakes were man-made floating islands of reeds tied
together and covered with soil. They appeared as floating
gardens whose plants' roots reached the reeds to feed directly
on the waters of the lakes.

The other Aztecs seen outside the valley were for the most
part military families who had been sent into subject lands to
strengthen the Aztec rule and provide warriors if trouble
threatened. But the valley was the heart of the Mexicas, the
place where its life source came from. This would have to be
destroyed if the Aztecs were to be conquered.

As Casca went from one place to another, content for a time
to wait, another felt that time was running out for him. Moctezuma was confused and worried. In the last few days he had
received more reports about the Spanish and their actions. He
had the feeling that fate was taking sides against him, forcing
him into patterns over which he had no control.

And what was he to do about this scar-faced one who had
followed his nephews back to his city? He had punished his
nephews by exiling them from the city. But now there were

these constant wanderings of the stranger. His men had reported back to him how Casca was looking everywhere, going
to temples and markets, watching the people as they went
about their everyday life. This was troubling the king. He had
just been told that the stranger was leaving Texcoco, where he
had been for the last two days, and heading out into the countryside, taking the old road that led to Teotihuacan. Why did
he wish to go there? The city was visited only by some priests
who went to inspect the shrine of the Quetzalcoatl, making an
occasional sacrifice in his name to honor the spirits of the
original builders.

CHAPTER THIRTEEN

The way to Teotihuacan was filled with memories that surged back to the front of Casca's mind after centuries of being buried. When they returned, it was as if they had happened only yesterday. The faces of those he had known, loved, and killed walked with him. Teypeytal, monstrous king of the Olmecs who resembled one of the ugly idols they worshiped, had died at his hand near this spot. As he entered the lane leading to the temple of the sun, he looked up at the pyramid where he had lain under the knife of the old priest Tezmec.

The old priest had been a good man, kind to children, gentle and greatly loved by his people. He'd had no desire for wealth or power, only to serve his gods and city to the best of his ability. He was a kind, caring old man who believed that what he did in the name of the gods was holy and right. When Casca put a stop to the practice of offering up the hearts of humans to the gods, Tezmec had offered himself up to his gods, sacrificing himself on the same altar on which he had sacrificed others.

The sun was setting as he reached the house where he had lived with Meta. He had loved her, and because of his love, he had tried to give her life beyond that of mortals; in trying, he had given her a horrible death. There were others, good and evil, whom he could see as if in a fog.

All that night, until just before dawn, he wandered the dead city, wondering what had happened to those he had left behind. His guards wearily kept him in sight, though they did give him some breathing space. They could feel that he was not trying to get away from them. Something important to him was taking place in this city of memories.

The captain of his guard was used to his charge acting in a strange manner and doing things that he should have had no knowledge of. It didn't bother him too much that Casca seemed to know his way around the city, making turns and entering deserted structures, never taking a path that didn't lead to where it seemed he wanted to go. But when Casca went to the place of the masks and found that the doors were intact and sealed, he turned to the guard and asked, "Are they still here? The masks?"

The guard felt a sudden chill and a desire to empty his bladder.

For his charge to know of the existence of the masks of the kings of Teotihuacan was one thing, but to know where they were kept in a city that he couldn't have been in before was something else.

Casca stayed in the city for three days, not speaking any more to the guards who never answered his questions. He knew the answer to his last one anyway; just from the shocked expression on the warrior's dark, painted face. From that moment on he gave no further indication that he even knew of his guards' presence. They didn't matter for they belonged to a living world and the one he was walking in was for the dead, the long dead, as he should have been centuries before.

When he went unerring to the room beneath the temple of the sun where the masks had been kept when first he walked these streets, the captain of his guard thought for a fleeting moment about trying to stop him. But Casca's face and the warning he'd had from Tenochtitlán not to interfere with him were incentives enough to leave the man alone. But he wasn't alone, others walked with him as he neared the dank musty confines below the ancient temple which was not as old as he. He groped his way blindly through a couple of turns along blackened corridors until the faint glow of an oil lamp beckoned him on as if he were a moth.

This was a sacred place with no need for permanent guards, only the priests who came periodically to service the lamps and make sacrifice to the masks had courage enough to enter these rooms unbidden. At the far end of the hall next to the last mask, he saw that which he sought. His mask of blue-green jade, carved by Pletuc, master cutter of the Teotec. His own face stared back at him from a row of ancient god-kings. The last mask was a face which looked vaguely familiar, then he recognized the features. It was that of Tezmec, the boy who had grown into a king. Now he was dust as were all the others of the thousands who had walked these dead streets. There had been much blood spilled on the altar stones before he came to rule, but not nearly as much as was wantonly spilled by the Aztecs. He left the chamber to regain the darkened boulevards of the city, leaving his other self behind, curiosity satisfied. The images of men and women going to their deaths those centuries past went with him. But there was no comparison between those who had died then, to even the twenty-five thousand who had gone under the sacrificial dagger to celebrate Moctezuma's ascendance to the throne of the Mexicas. He was, for the first time in longer than he could recall, truly shocked. Twenty-five thousand bleeding, burning hearts were offered up, and then the bodies were fed to the people.

As he walked through the cities of the lakes, the signs of sacrifice and the Aztecs' fascination with death were demonstrated everywhere. From the painted murals on the houses, the gods leered with horrible countenances as they claimed their victims. Many of their idols were made of clay and blood, and all needed blood to feed on. The Aztecs, as noble as they were in some respects, were a nation washed in the blood of others.

They would have to be stopped. He didn't know if what replaced them would be any better, but it could hardly be worse. Tens of thousands would have to die before that could take place, but then, tens of thousands were dying every year on the altars. Their lives were weights balancing against each other. Thousands now or thousands later?

If he was going to make the dying easier and quicker, he would have to see Moctezuma. There was the key to the power of the Aztecs. From the manner in which the Indians had greeted them and from the words he had overheard, he knew that in their minds there was a question and a great fear as to what the Spaniards were. Many believed that they were the gods returning from the sea to reclaim their lands, as had been foretold.

That was the key—to use the fear of their own gods as the tool to bring them down. But it was not yet time. Casca knew that Cortes had to consolidate his strength and make alliances among the nations that were hostile to or envious of the Aztecs. With his tiny force of six hundred men, there was no way that he could conquer the Aztecs, unless they had the help of the other tribes. This, together with the Aztecs' fears and superstitions, would be their main weapon. Then perhaps the Spanish could win and do it within a few months.

He had to wait. If Cortes moved and gained strength, Moctezuma would call Casca to him. It would be best now to let the king of the Aztecs ask him to come. When that happened, the time would be right for him to proclaim himself as the god returned, and then prove it. Until then, he would stay here, clean out some rooms, and move in. This would be his home as it had been before. Moctezuma would call him one day. It might be months before he did, but he would call him. It was his destiny.

Casca's guards were not thrilled with his taking up residence in the city of the gods, for this was not a place for men to live. Only the priests came here now or the coyotes that made dens for their pups under the blocks of the temple of the moon. Sometimes the cough of a hunting jaguar could be heard as it prowled the outskirts of the city in search of prey, but they seldom entered the city to where the walls of the temples loomed. The place still smelled of man and death. The cats preferred the cleaner hunting grounds of the jungles or deserts.

The daily reports of the activities of the scar-faced one were still made. The news of his new residence gave Moctezuma several nightmares in which the gods rejected his offer of self-sacrifice, thus condemning him and casting him out of their favor. And it was always the Feathered Serpent on his throne who sat in judgment of him, gray-blue eyes blazing behind a death mask of jade.

The winter storms came to the deserts. Dark clouds moved inland, boiling in from the seas and forests to feed the desert and make it bloom. Still Casca never left the city, save to walk a bit in the fields.

He waited patiently as only one such as he could. Time, he had been told, was a great circle, a wheel that constantly turned on itself. He merely had to wait for the wheels of eternity to turn long enough. Here, in this timeless place, he almost felt at peace as he moved silently among the ancient structures that were nearly as old as he.

When he tried to speak with his guards, they would answer only in the shortest of sentences. They did not like this man or god; he was not of their world. They brought him food and supplies. Once, at the king's command, they even brought him a selection of beautiful young girls to pick from. He could have had one or all of them, but he just smiled sadly and sent them away. It was to their great relief, for they feared him more than the warriors did.

The priest who first met him came to watch him from time to time. With each visit, he grew to hate the pale one more and more, although he could not say why.

During the storms of winter, Moctezuma could restrain his own curiosity no longer and visited the City of the Gods disguised as a member of his own bodyguard. He watched Casca's wanderings and took note of his silence. He was fascinated, drawn to yet frightened of the man. Moctezuma had planned on returning to Tenochtitlán before dark, but he couldn't leave; he had to see more. He had to try to understand what this man was and what he wanted. Before the night was over, he would wish that he had returned rather than witness the events of that stormy night.

Casca, as had become his habit when nightfall came, went to the Pyramid of the Sun, climbed to the top, and rested on the altar, which was still dark from the blood of thousands of "messengers." Moctezuma stayed at the halfway point, where he had a good view of both the top and the altar. He wrapped his cotton robe about his shoulder and waited, yet he did not know for what. But something was in the air, riding in on the storm clouds. Lightning crackled in the distance, coming close to Teotihuacan. The thunder rode the skies, rolling across the floor of the desert and turning it dark. Even under the light of the full moon, the shadows swirled and converged, growing stronger and darker, broken only by the bolts of lightning and the cracks of thunder echoing through valleys and mountains. The chill grew greater, but he waited, as did the man on the altar.

Casca's mind leaped back, the smell of the storm and lightning returning him to that distant time when he had been prepared for the altar. He felt the stifling heat of the jade mask on his face, carved in his likeness by Pletuc, master carver of the Teotec.

Once more he walked the two miles to the Pyramid of the Quetza, the one the Aztecs called the temple of the sun. But then it had been the Quetza's. Two miles, every step accompanied by the beat of drums and the shrill trilling of flutes as he advanced. His scarred body was covered by a priceless robe of woven feathers that were green. On his head was a serpent headdress, the mouth open, the fangs ready. The eyes were made of red precious stones that gleamed malevolently. He took each step with the beat of his heart. The coca leaves he had eaten had begun to take effect as he moved into the heat waves rising over the floor of stones leading to the altar, shimmering and alive.

Tezmec, the high priest, had led the way past the streets lined with all the people of the valley, who had come to witness and participate in this most holy of events. A messenger was to be sent to the gods to take them their prayers and bring the life-giving rains and good fortune to the city and its subjects. Tens of thousands watched him as he passed.

Something was happening. Moctezuma shook his head and rubbed his eyes as he watched the man on the altar. He was moving, holding his arms and head in a strange manner. Moctezuma thought he was having a vision. For a moment he seemed to see the man in a serpent headdress and feathered ceremonial robe, the streets filled with images. It passed, and then it returned, this time in startling clarity. Moctezuma was witnessing something that had happened before and was occurring again, but only he and the stranger were there. Where did all the others come from? The old priest with his ceremonial dagger of obsidian, the thousands on the streets? And did he hear the faded beat of skin tambors, or was it the approaching storm clouds? He watched, unable to tear his eyes away. What he saw was not the man on the top of the pyramid. He saw another in the stranger's image who even now was laying his body down on the altar, exposing his chest for the fatal blow by the aged priest of the Serpent.

The storm clouds broke, thunder crashed, and the knife of the priest fell, striking into the chest of the messenger. Swiftly, with practiced hands, the priest removed the heart of the sacrifice and held it up for the thousands in the streets below to witness and honor. The storm erupted over the city and centered on the temple. Moctezuma whimpered as he saw what happened next. The sacrifice sat up at the altar, his chest a gaping, draining, ragged wound. The sacrifice reached out his hand, reclaiming his own beating heart from the hand of the priest, and then rose from the altar.

The wind screamed like a wounded woman, piercing the senses. Moctezuma fell to his knees as he saw the phosphorescent glow from the skies. Green and shining, it fell upon the altar and its victim as he stood, his still beating heart in his hand, glowing with the green fire of heaven. The messenger raised his voice over the storm. Moctezuma's mind nearly broke as he heard words that were last spoken over a thousand years before rip at his consciousness. The man-god cried out, "Look and see that which none has seen before!" The ghostly thousands and Moctezuma obeyed, and they watched as he took his own heart and returned it to his chest.

"I am the Quetza!" he cried. Then he put his hands on both sides of his chest and pushed the edges of the wound together, closing the gaping hole.

Moctezuma wept as he saw the wound close and rivulets of blood run down the messenger's chest to flow onto the stones and drip down the steps. Above the roar of the storm, he saw Casca raise his arms to the heavens and cry out in pain and anguish.

"I, Casca. I am the Quetza!"

Moctezuma tried to cover his ears but couldn't as the last words tore at the very fabric of his soul. The man on the altar, his body burning with the green fire, screamed again and drowned out the thunder of the skies with his words:

"I am God!"

Moctezuma fainted. When he awoke, his guards were carrying him in a litter back to his palace. When he questioned them as to what they had seen that night, they looked at him in confusion, not knowing what was wanted from them. They could only answer honestly. "We saw nothing, our lord, only you and the strange man sitting on the altar of the sun. You watched him for a few minutes and then fainted. That is all we saw, nothing more save the storm."

Moctezuma never returned to the City of the Gods. That now belonged to the scarred one and his magic. Now more than ever, he feared those from the sea. What should he do? What could he do? They were coming. He could not keep them away forever. They were coming for him even now.

Cortes questioned his new allies about the disappearance of his man known as Carlos Romano. They knew nothing. There had been rumors that one such as he had been seen heading west across the trails leading to the high deserts. But that was all. The subjects of the Aztecs were not speaking. A silence had fallen between them and their subject and vassal tribes.

Cortes had the feeling that Romano was up to something, but what it could be he couldn't even guess at. One man was not important enough to cause him to have a major confrontation with the Aztecs. Whatever Romano was up to, he had a feeling it would not be to the advantage of the Indians. There was an odd quality about the man. Just what it was, he couldn't put into words, but there was definitely something.

Cortes shook the thought off. He had more pressing matters to worry over than the whereabouts of one man. He had an entire country to conquer for the glory of Spain and himself.

CHAPTER FOURTEEN

Cortes had spent the last months fortifying his new city of Vera Cruz to make it secure from attack and building alliances among his neighbors. Soon it would be time to move against the city of the Mexicas. Then he would not be denied his meeting with the king of the Aztecs.

It was not long after the nephews of Moctezuma had left that the Cempolans asked Cortes for help in destroying the Culhuan, who were one of the few willing vassals of the Aztecs. They had a garrison at Tizapantzinco, a fortress built on a rocky butt near a river on the border between the lands of the Totonacs and those of the Cempolans.

When the Culhuans there found the countryside in revolt and their tax collectors attacked, they sent their warriors out in strength, raiding the villages and towns within their reach, putting them all to the torch and taking captives for the altars. Cortes decided that it would be good to reinforce his new allies' faith in him, and so he agreed to go with them the two days' journey, taking with him a hundred foot soldiers and fifty horses.

When they reached the base of the butt, he held his Spaniards back, letting the Cempolans go out first to show themselves and hurl challenges at the Culhuans, who reacted predictably, sallying out in full strength to destroy the impudent Cempolans. Once they were committed and fully exposed, Cortes set loose his Spaniards on them, his cavalry cutting off the Culhuans from their city. The natives panicked when they saw the Spaniards; they had never laid eyes on white men or horses before. They broke and ran for the trees and river with the Cempolans hot on their trail. Cortes took four of his officers and climbed the butt to the gates of Tizapantzinco, holding it with no difficulty until the main force of Cempolans and Spaniards could enter.

He turned the city over to his allies after making them promise not to hurt the civilians there. They were to disarm their prisoners and then set them free. This was a strange thing for the Indians to do, as they never released captives, but they obeyed his wishes. As usual, Cortes had reasons for everything he did. He wanted the survivors of the Culhuan force to go out into the countryside and spread his fame. They would let the world of the Aztecs know that he was not to be resisted. At the same time, he would gain the support of several other tribes, including those of the other Culhuan cities.

One other bit of good news awaited his return to Vera Cruz. A friend of his from Cuba had arrived with a caravel carrying sixty good soldiers and nine horses, which were worth more than fifty men each because of the effect they had on the Indians.

Upon his return, he called for a meeting of his town leaders, the alcaldes and regidores. The treasure they had acquired to this date was brought into the square of the City of the True Cross and displayed for all to see. Besides the small things of cotton and feather works, which had no real value other than their craftsmanship, the gold and silver they had gained was valued at twenty-seven thousand ducats.

It was time for him to renew the loyalty of his men and buy the favor of his king. He told the council to distribute the wealth among the men after deducting the king's fifth share and then said that he would take only his fair share as captain general of the expedition, not deducting at this time his costs for the ships and supplies he'd had to pay for. He wanted his men to have their shares in full so that they might pay off any debts they had accrued in order to join his forces.

Among the king's share were sent the two disks of gold and

silver that had been given to him by Tuedilli. Also on the list was a necklace of gold with eighty-three small emeralds set in it and another of four twisted strands of gold with one hundred and two rubies and a hundred and seventy-two emeralds. These and many other items, some of gold or silver, others of pearls and gems, and many articles of native clothing that showed the incredibly beautiful work of the Indian craftsmen in cloth and feathers were all included on the list.

As he prepared his gifts, there were many men being held by the Cempolans as sacrifices. Even he had not been able to halt their practices completely and was wise enough to wait and try to convince them through other arguments later. The best he could do was to get the Cempolans to release four of the sacrifices to his custody and send them along with the treasure to Spain under the watchful eyes of two trusted deputies, Alonso de Ortocarrero and Francisco de Montejo. They carried the treasure and his letter, requesting his highness to proclaim officially that Cortes was, in the king's name, to be governor of the lands he had delivered to the throne of Spain.

The ship left Vera Cruz on July 26, 1519, making certain they avoided Havana and the power of Diego Velasquez. Cortes's old enemy, who was lieutenant governor of Cuba, would have taken the ship and gained the credit for winning the treasure for himself.

Even in the camp of Cortes, there were some who were more loyal to Diego than they were to Cortes and attempted to spread sedition, saying that Cortes had made himself leader by bribes and trickery and that Diego was the legitimate authority of the new lands, just as he was of Cuba.

Cortes responded quickly, arresting the ringleaders and holding them prisoner on board ship. Some time later, when he thought things had calmed down a bit, he released them. But they started to give him trouble again. Cortes discovered that they were plotting to seize a brigantine, kill its master, and sail to Cuba to inform Diego Velasquez of what Cortes was attempting to do and of the treasure ship he had sent to Spain.

For the first time, Cortes had to act against his own men. After a quick trial, he hanged Juan Escudero and the pilot Diego Cermeno and had several others whipped. These actions did nothing to reduce the respect that his men held for him, for men of strength respect strength.

After this, he knew that it was time for him to move on again so that there would be less time for any of them to consider such treason again. He would wait no longer; it was time to enter the heartland of the Aztecs.

He was concerned about the men he would have to leave behind to garrison Vera Cruz. When he was not there, who could tell what would happen to them or the actions they might be seduced into taking by the fearful and weak of spirit? From history, he recalled the actions of Alexander when he landed on the coast of Persia. He burned his ships, leaving his men no choice but to go forward and in the process found a great empire.

After removing their guns, sails, ropes, and anything else that could be of use, he sank his ships. There was some grumbling over this, but he soothed their feelings with stories of the prizes they would take, which would make them all as rich as princes. The words were sweet, and the Spaniards had no choice in the matter. For now they had no way to return, and without Cortes's leadership and influence over the Indians, they knew that their chances of survival would be reduced severely. They would go with him all the way to the City of Mexico and beyond.

He left Vera Cruz to the care of Pedro de Ircio, who owed his life to his captain. Pedro would be secure with his men at hand and the fifty thousand warriors he could draw upon from his Indian allies.

Cortes returned to Cempola. When he left this time, he had convinced their king to cast down his idols and take up the true cross as his symbol, promising him that if they did this, they would have his continued support against the Aztecs, although he might remove that support if they did not. Tazcamili gave him a thousand men as porters and several hostages of noble blood as tokens of his good faith, which Cortes willingly accepted. The porters would be used to haul the heavy guns and provisions, leaving his men with little to wear them down, save their personal weapons and armor.

After giving Cempola the new name of Sevilla, he began his march to Mexico, leading four hundred Spaniards, fifteen horses, three small guns, and three hundred Indian warriors, including several nobles.

The march had begun. Once they left the fertile lands of the coast behind, they entered a barren and sterile land where the water was bad, tasting of strong salts. For three days they had to pass through this region to reach the mountain valley of Zacotlan, a vassal state of Moctezuma ruled over by Olintetl, a noble lord who thought that the Spaniards must be friends of his master. To honor the occasion of their arrival, he sacrificed fifty men, an act which the Spaniards were hard put not to stop with some killing of their own. From the lord Olintetl, Cortes learned that there were regular garrisons of five thousand warriors spread out in stations all the way to Tenochtitlán, and Moctezuma had thirty vassal lords, each of whom had one hundred thousand warriors at his command and countless lesser lords such as himself who could muster only twenty or thirty thousand. Each year they sacrificed twenty thousand men and women, a fact he boasted of, for it proved the piety of the Aztecs. At special times it could go as high as fifty thousand.

Cortes had known that Moctezuma was a great king, but not to this extent. If Olintetl was telling the truth, and there was no reason to believe otherwise, the Aztecs could field three million warriors, a larger army than even the greatest kings of Europe could command. If he had been a lesser man, he would have turned back, satisfied with his gains; but he was committed, and now he would use a lesson not from Alexander but from Caeser in order to win. He would divide and conquer, trusting, as he had with the Cempolans, that there were still many more of the subject states that could be brought over to his side with the promise of independence and aid—that and the fact that the communications were so poor in a land with no horses. He could strike and be at the next place before word of his actions could be acted on by the enemy.

He moved on, leaving Olintetl thinking that he was their good friend, and rapidly went into action, taking on first the Tlaxcalans, one of the few independent neighbors of the Aztecs who ruled themselves, paying no tribute to any lords but their own. If he could beat them, he would have a much better chance of making the lesser tribes his willing partners.

It was a hard fight in which he lost two horses and had a number of his men wounded, but once again the Good Lord was with them and no Spaniards died in battle. He wondered how long his luck could hold. The Cempolans and his other allies fought bravely. It was very doubtful that the Spaniards could have won on their own. By the first week of September, they had defeated the Tlaxcalan armies, who had boasted that they would sacrifice the strangers to their gods and feast on "heavenly flesh," as they called human meat. Possibly they might have dined on the Castilians, if not for the cannon and the horses, which had their usual effect on the savages.

In the last battle, The Tlaxcalans' pride and arrogance were nearly overbearing, for they mocked the Spaniards and their allies, saying: "What fools and contemptible men are these, who threaten us without knowing our strength, who dare to come to our lands without our permission and against our will." When the Tlaxcalans saw that the Spanish were fatigued, they laughed and made sport, saying: "Let them rest, for we shall have time to take and tie them. Send them food, lest they claim they were weak from hunger as the reason that we were able to take them." And they did send food to their enemy, who consumed it eagerly.

The Tlaxcalans, as with all the Indians of the new lands, made at least one critical error in their fighting techniques. The Indians fought to take captives for their altars. There was not as much glory in killing a man as in taking him alive. The Spanish and their allies were not bothered by such conventions. They killed and killed only, as Cortes ordered them.

The Tlaxcalans were well equipped with shields and armor of wood and leather, spears and lances, bows and arrows, the flint or obsidian-lined *macama*, and swords of hard wood. They painted their faces bright scarlet, looking like red-faced, feathered devils.

The fighting lasted over a week, and every day at the same time the Tlaxcalans would send food to their enemy. The last time, they also sent spies with the servants who delivered the food. These were sent back to their masters with their hands cut off.

Every day it was the turn of a different Tlaxcalan army to do battle with the Spanish, and every day it was the same result. The enemy still held the field, and they had lost many more than the strangers. If the Tlaxcalans had used their forces in concert instead of piecemeal, they would have had little trouble eliminating the invaders. But each detachment was under the command of its own chieftain who did not wish to share his glory with any other.

They bled themselves dry and accomplished nothing until superstitious fear began to ride their thoughts, growing greater in their minds with each failure until they began to believe that their gods had deserted them. Once this happened, it was only a matter of days before messengers came to the Spanish camp, pleading for a treaty in which most of the Tlaxcalan cities would swear to be the good and great friends of the Spaniards and their king.

Cortes granted this, as he did not wish to tie up his men in fighting the Tlaxcalans. They would be needed later in Mexico. He made his treaty and gained another two thousand porters and a thousand warriors to add to his force. After their treaty, Cortes used his tactic of gentle treatment to make them into allies. As with most savages, once it was proved who was their better, they readily accepted whoever sat upon their necks as their lords.

Cortes's confidence was not shared by all his men, who, once they saw the tenacity of the Tlaxcalans and their numbers, began to grumble, afraid that they would never get back alive. The rumors began to spread until Cortes had to draw his company together away from the Indians and speak to them.

He stroked his beard as he looked over his soldiers, watching their eyes and body movements. He just waited, watching, saying nothing until they started shuffling their feet in embarrassment. Then he began, his voice strong and confident:

"Gentlemen and friends, I chose you as my companions and you chose me as your captain for the service of God and the increase of His holy faith and also for the service of our king and even for our own profit. I, as you have observed, have not failed or offended you; nor indeed have you done so to me up to this point. Now, however, I sense a weakening among some of you and a little taste to finish the war we have on our hands, a war which, with the help of God, we have now concluded. At least we now know how little harm it can do us. We have partly seen the good we shall gain from it, although what you shall see henceforth will be greater beyond comparison, so much so that it passes my thought and words. Fear not, my companions, to come with me, for never yet have

Spaniards been afraid in these new lands which by their courage, strength, and cunning they have conquered and discovered; nor do I entertain such a thought of you. God forbid that I should think or that anyone should believe that my Spaniards would be afraid or disobedient to their captain! One must never turn one's back on the enemy, lest it appear to be a retreat. There is no retreat or, to put it more mildly, no withdrawal which does not bring grief to those who make it, for they shall know shame, hunger, loss of friends and their wealth and arms, and lastly death, which is not the worst of them, for infamy endures forever.''

He paused to watch the effect of his words. Satisfied that he had them where he wanted them, he pressed on:

''If we abandon this country, this war, this adventure that we have undertaken, and turn back, then shall we not lose our honor? Did you think that in another place you would find easier wealth and fewer enemies?

''Never since we came to this land have we, thank God, lacked for food and friends, gold and honor. You can see how these people hold you to be more than mortal men, almost gods. With all their numbers and arms, they have not succeeded in slaying a single one of you. Now listen to me. We have no way back. Ahead of us is Mexico, where Moctezuma resides among riches impossible to calculate. Persevere and we shall have it all: serfs and vassals to do our bidding, gold, silver, precious gems, pearls, and above all, the honor due us from the rest of the world as Spaniards. The greater the king, the greater the enemy, the greater the land, so much greater shall be our glory.

''So then have no fear, and never doubt our final victory, for most of the distance is behind you. You have vanquished the Tlaxcalans, who numbered over a hundred thousand warriors and are said to be as fierce as the Aztecs. With the help of God we shall finish off the few who still oppose us and march on to the final glory for our god, our king, and Spain!''

The conquistadors roared their approval until their faces turned red and sweaty under their steel helmets. Now if one wished to speak of turning back, he could do it only at the risk of his life. Cortes had turned their fears into courage and lust for the wealth of Mexico, and they would not be denied. They were ready to move on ever closer to the heartland of the

greatest of the Indian kingdoms and the most elusive treasure
of all—Moctezuma!

Among those who cheered the loudest was Juan de Castro.
He had the beginnings of a full dark beard and had put on
weight since Casca had walked off. The life of a conquistador
suited him, and he had gained the respect of his peers for
courage and swordplay. He now belonged with the elite
caballeros who had horses. As he was known to have been the
missing man's sword-mate, there were no objections when he
was given his horse. Juan no longer believed that his absent
compadre would return. He had paid the priests to say a mass
for him and had lit candles in his name.

CHAPTER FIFTEEN

Moctezuma tried to hide the truth of their coming, but at last he knew that he could not resist his fate any further, especially when his chamberlain told him, "My king, they are coming. They have defeated the Tlaxcalans without the loss of a man and have made them their servants, adding the forces of the Tlaxcalan to their own. They have only yesterday destroyed Cholula, putting its people to the sword when they resisted them."

Moctezuma nearly wept as his chamberlain continued his tale of woe. "Oh, my king, they are the most terrible beings, with their strange weapons of thunder and fire and their small bows that can send an arrow completely through the body of a strong man and have enough power to kill another behind him. My lord, they must be gods.

"The Cholutecas resisted them, as they have long been enemies of the Tlaxcalans. They put their faith in the god Quetzalcoatl. They made magic and cast spells and sent warnings to these 'gods' to pass them by, for they were not as weak as the sodomite Tlaxcalans, who are now no more than women for the use of the 'gods.' "

His chamberlain shivered with the impact of his own words. "They were very brave, my king, to resist with such courage

119

those from the sea. They told the strangers that they were protected by the great god Queztalcoatl. The priests promised the
'gods' that if they came to Cholula, they would be destroyed
by bolts of fire from the heavens and the Pyramid of the God
would open up to pour forth rivers of water to drown them as
though they were rats in a jar.

"To protect themselves from drowning, priests scraped
away the surface layer of the pyramid to let loose the waters.
Then they made great magic by making a mortar by mixing the
blood from children of two or three years of age with lime.
With this they would be able to plug up the holes from which
the floods of the god would come.

"In their pride and confidence, they met the envoy who
served the 'gods,' a chief of the Tlaxcalans named Patlhuat-
zin. Their answer to his pleas for peace and welcome for the
'gods' was to flay the skin from his face and arms. His hands
they cut so that they dangled by strips of skin from his wrists,
and they sent him back as their response."

At this news Moctezuma could not restrain a moan of fear.
Envoys and messengers had always had priviliged status and
were not to be hurt or killed.

Dropping to his knees, with his hands covering his eyes, his
chamberlain finished the tale of Cholula. "When this was
done, the 'gods' and their traitor allies came forth to do battle.
Their weapons of white iron cut through those of Cholula as if
they were made of green reeds. Their fierce dogs savaged all
they could reach, and their weapons shot fire and thunder into
the houses of the gods, killing many. When the priests attempted to let loose the flood of the god, it did not come. Nor
was there fire from heaven to strike down the pale ones. The
god Quetza had turned his face from them, and in their
despair, hundreds committed suicide by throwing themselves
head first from the top of the temples to the stones, smashing
their brains out. Great was the slaughter of the Cholutecas,
and their city was put to the torch and plundered. Cholula is
no more, my king!"

Tears ran down the face of Moctezuma. Had the god turned
his face because they had broken the old laws of the people of
Teotihuacan and made human sacrifice? Were the pale ones
the manifestations of the god or just his servants? And what
of the scar-faced one who waited in the City of the Gods to see

him? He was not as other men.

At last Moctezuma could not put it off any longer. He told his chamberlain to rise. "Go to Teotihuacan and say to the pale one there that I wish to see him. Take him gifts of gold and silver, for pale ones love these things greatly, and ask him to come to me with all haste, for we have much to speak of."

The chamberlain bowed his way back out to do his master's bidding, though he did not like it. His king was on the ragged edge of panic.

Casca was brought to the Aztec king in his private chambers. His retainers and servants were dismissed, leaving the two men facing each other. Moctezuma was wondering what he was going to say to the scar-faced man. The ice was broken by Casca when he spoke to him in the Nahual tongue:

"Tectli, I have returned, true to my words spoken those centuries ago when I ruled as lord of Teotihuacan." Casca moved closer to the king. "Is not my mask still in its resting place in the hall at the base of the temple of the serpent? Have you looked upon its face? If so, then look at mine!"

Moctezuma covered his eyes, remembering the night on the pyramid and the vision in the storm. "No," he cried. "You cannot be he whose coming was foretold." He forced himself to look at the stranger's face, examining it inch by inch. There was a resemblance. He still tried to fight the proof of his senses and forced out the words, "I must have more than a memory and a dream." Moctezuma cried out for the priest Ceypal to be brought to him. As they waited, Casca could see the fear that was eating the heart of the king.

He didn't want to believe the legend, but too many things were pointing to its reality—though not in the manner in which he had thought it would come true. But who could say what guise the gods would take in their schemes? They were not bound by the rules of mortal men.

A thin voice begging permission to enter into the presence of the king came to them through the closed door. Moctezuma spoke as firmly as he could, granting the request. Ceypal entered, his body painted black, his hair bedraggled, his garb stained with the clotted blood of a recent sacrifice. His face was freshly painted with circles of red and white around the eyes, and a black band ran from the mouth to each ear.

It offended Casca that this one could rip out the living heart of a man, woman, or child and think it a good and holy thing to do. Looking at him made the blood in his temples pound a bit harder.

The priest looked at Casca with ill-concealed hatred and loathing. Moctezuma ordered Ceypal, "Go now to the hall of the masks and bring with all haste the sacred mask of the Quetza." Ceypal bowed his way out of the royal presence, but not before grinning at Casca as if to say, "Soon I will have your body bent over the altar block and your heart in my hand."

Moctezuma tried to be as controlled and polite as possible, offering his guest food and drink, both of which were refused. He noticed for the first time that his guest wore no jewels or gold, no robe of many feathers, only his plain armor of white iron and his sword. Had his orders been disobeyed and the scar-faced one not been sent the presents as he had commanded?

"Were you not given gifts by my command?" he asked.

Casca nodded his head. "Yes, they brought me many things of great beauty and value, but I have no need for them. I have not come here for gold or silver. I have come for something far more important than that."

Moctezuma wondered what it was that could be more important than that which the rest of his kind seemed to hunger after with such a passion.

Casca found a place by the window where the breeze was cool; he could see the lake on which the city was built. Temple fires were burning like many scattered beacons, the lights blazing across the lake from the cities of Texcoco and Huexotla. He knew that those lights meant that offerings were being made and blood was being spilled even as he and the king waited. Keeping his back to the king, he spoke, his voice very soft, in a tone one would sometimes use when chiding a disobedient but well-loved child.

"Why did you not obey my laws? The smell of death hangs over the land like a cloud of blood."

Moctezuma said nothing, but he suddenly remembered the death of Cholula, who had sacrificed in the name of the Serpent. The manner of the man's speaking bothered him more than anything else. The scarred one spoke as one who was recalling things long past.

Casca moved away from the window, turning to face the king. His skin reddened from the glow of the torches in their brackets. He nearly whispered as he spoke. "The old ones of the City of the Gods told your father's father of me, didn't they? They told you also of my law that no more human blood was to be spilled upon the altars of this land or disaster would surely follow. Death would walk your streets, and your nation would be cast down." Casca covered his eyes as if the visions he was seeing in his mind were too painful. "You should have listened, for now it is too late. If I had seen that you had obeyed my laws, then I would have stopped those who are even now bringing to you the death of your nation."

Moctezuma couldn't know that by his words, Casca had meant that if the people of Mexico had been better than the Catholic invaders, he would have killed Cortes, without whose leadership the rest would have fled this land and returned to the safety of Cuba. At least they would have fled for a time, but in that time he could have shown the Aztecs how to use their great wealth to deal with the Spaniards, how to play one side against the other and make the best use of their gold to buy the services of those in Europe who could have kept their nation free. It was too late now. What Casca had witnessed on his way to Tenochtitlán and what he had seen in the months since his arrival had made his choice for him.

As bad as the conquistadors were, the Aztecs were worse in the long run. A minimum of twenty thousand a year were taken to the altars. It was too much for him to defend, and the other nations—the Chichimecs and Culhuans, Zapotecas and Tlaxcalans, these and others he had not yet heard of—all sent their offerings to the gods. It had to stop. The best thing he could do was make the death song of the Aztecs as short as possible by convincing Moctezuma that there was no way to resist that which was coming.

Moctezuma could find no words; he sat on a cushion of soft leather and waited. His guest returned to his place by the window and watched him. Casca looked at the face of Moctezuma, a gentle, intelligent face, dark and handsome. He was a well-built man with no trace of overt cruelty about him. What Moctezuma did, he did from a sense of duty and devotion. He was not a cruel man by nature, no more than were the priests of the Inquisition. What they did also was out of faith.

The two waited, each busy with his own thoughts. It would be nearly dawn before Ceypal could make it back from Teotihuacan with the mask of the Quetzalcoatl. For both of them the hours were unnaturally long.

The first streaks of the sun had glanced over the waters of Texcoco when Ceypal returned to the palace, carrying a chest of dark wood wrapped with red cloth. This he gave over to his king. Moctezuma carefully and with trembling hands unwrapped the cloth, pausing before he opened the chest. Casca could see the large vein in the king's neck throbbing. Slowly, Moctezuma removed the mask from the chest. He set it on a table of carved dark wood and leather. Taking an oil lamp, he held the flame close to the mask. Ceypal stood back in contempt, hatred written all over his face. He was barely able to control an outburst, demanding that his king give the stranger to him and stop this charade.

Casca moved to the table. Taking the mask from the hands of the king, he held it up by his face so that both he and the mask were staring at Moctezuma. The king nearly broke. They were the same—the same blue-gray eyes and the scar. Everything was the same! The god or his manifestation was standing before him.

The priest Ceypal could see his lord falling apart and could not restrain himself any longer. "My lord king, it is a trick of some kind. True, there is a resemblance between this man and the mask, but that is all there is. He is a mortal man the same as you and I. If he is cut, will he not bleed? If his heart is torn from his body, will he not die?"

Casca grinned, his teeth reflecting the light of the lamp. He set the jade mask back on the table and answered the priest's questions.

"No!" He smiled. "I will not!" Baring one thickly muscled arm, he reached over to Ceypal, taking the ceremonial dagger from him before the priest could protest. Holding the translucent, serrated blade in his hand, he repeated the priest's questions. "You said, 'If he is cut, will he not bleed?' " Casca drew the blade along the inside of his arm, laying the meat open until blood ran freely. Ceypal gloated at the sight of blood on the stranger's arm.

"See," he cried. "He bleeds!" Moctezuma moved closer to examine the wound. As he did, Casca wiped the blood from his arm, exposing the cut. Moctezuma flinched. As he watched with unbelieving eyes, the wound healed itself. The edges closed together, and the bleeding stopped.

Casca continued, his voice hollow as death. "You said, priest, 'If his heart is torn from his body, will he not die?' To that the answer is also no!" He removed his breastplate and tunic, exposing his chest and arms to the lamp. The crisscrossing of scars and wounds was astonishing. Casca took the lamp, holding it close to his body. The deep scar in the center of his chest removed the last doubt from the mind of Moctezuma, for in his vision by the pyramid, he had seen that wound made and healed as the god reclaimed his beating heart from the hands of the priest who had cut it from him. He was the god returned.

Ceypal still tried to interrupt them with his protests. Casca was a bit tired of his interference. Placing the lamp on the table to rest beside his mask, he reached over with his right hand, grabbing Ceypal by the neck. He raised the priest off the floor until his feet no longer touched. Casca's face contorted with the effort as he concentrated on sending all his strength into his arm and fingers. Ceypal's face bulged under the pressure, swelling out. If it hadn't been painted already, it would have turned completely black as the thick fingers crushed into his flesh, cracking the vertebrae in the neck, crumbling his esophagus till not even Ceypal's death rattle could escape, much less the blood that was draining back down into his lungs. Casca gave the priest one last great shake, as a dog would a rat, and tossed the carcass to the floor.

Pointing a finger at the pale face of the Aztec king, he whispered, "Do not offend me further."

Moctezuma pulled his cloak over his head and fell to the floor on his face. Prostrate before the god, he sobbed out, "Mercy, Tectli Quetza. Have mercy on me and my people."

CHAPTER SIXTEEN

Moctezuma and Casca stayed in the king's chambers until past midday. Casca had to deliver his words carefully when Moctezuma asked what he should do.

Casca stood by the door thinking. He had made Moctezuma tell him all he knew about the Spaniards and what they were doing, including the slaughter of Cholula and the sacrifice of the children by the Cholutecas. Cortes was coming and was not far away.

"You must not oppose their coming any further, for if you do, all the tribes who are not your friends will ally themselves against you. Let Cortes come."

Moctezuma was too frightened to argue, but he was still confused. "But if you are the god, then who is the one called Cortes?"

Casca took his time. He knew more about the religion of the Aztecs and Indians of Mexico than any other of his race.

"I have many faces and many bodies. I can enter the soul of any I choose and use them as my tool. I am Cortes and a hundred others. You will treat him as you would me, for we are of the same spirit and use these fleshy shells only to serve our purpose. If they are destroyed, then I shall take another and another, for the spirit cannot be destroyed. I am going to leave

126

you for a time, but we shall meet again. Obey me and do not resist those who are coming."

Casca walked away from the palace and out across the causeway leading to Tlacopan. From there he took the road leading to the volcano Popocatepetl. Cortes would have to pass within view of the smoking mountain. He would wait there until he came; it should not be much longer.

What he was doing to Moctezuma was harsh, but it was the only chance he had to save the lives of tens of thousands. If Moctezuma gave over the control of the Aztec empire to Cortes, there would not be as much bloodshed. It would save the lives of both Indian and Spaniard and perhaps preserve the good things of the Aztec culture too.

For now he could do no more. He would just have to wait for the conquistadors to come to him.

Three days and nights passed as he waited and watched on the slopes of the volcano. During the day he would go down lower to where he could gather wood and brush to keep him warm in the thin air. For food he ate mostly dried corn and meat he had picked up at the market in Tlacopan. At night the volcano rumbled and smoked to keep him company. On the third night, he heard men coming up the rough slopes. From the manner in which they moved and the hush of their voices, he knew that they were searching for him and that they were not Castilians. If his fire hadn't gone out as he slept, they most likely would have found him by now. Wearily he put on his plain breastplate and unsheathed his sword. He wondered if Moctezuma had sent them but thought it unlikely. Hiding behind a boulder of volcanic slag, he waited and listened.

The Aztecs were not very quiet. Loose rocks and gravel gave away their movements. Moving to the side of the boulder, he saw them coming up. Leading them was a priest, his face painted black. He knew where this bit of trouble had originated. One of Ceypal's priestly order had taken it upon himself to seek vengeance. The six warriors with him were from the war god's Eagle Clan. In the lead, just in front of the priest, was a captain of the Eagles. Casca let him pass by, half crawling on hands and knees up the steep sides of the smoking mountain. This was no time for a sense of fair play or nobility. Casca was in no mood for it. He wanted to get it over with as quickly as possible.

The Eagle captain was only a few feet up from the boulder
when Casca rose, stepped forward two paces, and stabbed him
through the back, his long steel blade entering the warrior's
heart. Whipping his sword hand back around, he caught the
priest rising, half on his hands and knees. The sword sliced his
lower jaw off and then flicked back to open his throat. One
more of the remaining five Eagle warriors found his belly split
open by the Spanish steel. The last four turned and ran, racing
back down the hill, slipping and sliding. Without the priest
and their captain, they had no desire to meet the devil on the
mountain. By the time they reached the bottom of the volcano, they looked as if they had been in a major battle. Their
bodies were covered with cuts and scrapes from which blood
oozed. Casca let them go. He doubted that he would be
bothered anymore, but just to make sure, he moved his camp
to another place where it would be even more difficult for
anyone to come on him by surprise and he could still watch for
the army of Cortes. Idly he wondered how de Castro was far-
ing.

Cortes was ecstatic at the news the messengers from Moctezuma had brought him. The way was now open to Tenochtitlán and the heart of the Aztec empire. There would be no
further resistance.

The Spaniards and their army, which had grown to six thousand, marched with him. They were still cautious about ambush or treachery, which was well, for since the Spanish had
come, Moctezuma had done little to oppose them. The king
was not in favor with many of his military commanders. Kings
had been made before, and they could be broken if they went
against the will of their people, especially the clans of the
armies.

The conquistadors made Huejotzingo their camp after the
first day's march. The next day they reached a pass between
two snow-covered peaks from where they could look out over
the valley of Mexico. Its lakes and towns dotted the shores.
Cortes led the way down from the pass. He would be the first
to set foot in the valley. Once off the mountain, he made camp
at a large estate belonging to a prince of Mexico. It was large
enough so that his entire force was easily accommodated and
fed.

While the Spaniards were there, many nobles of Tenochtit-lán and other cities came to plead with him to go back, though they knew that Moctezuma had given orders that the strangers were not to be hindered in their advance. Cortes was promised tribute to be paid each year if he would return to the coast and go no farther. Cortes would have none of it. No matter how much gold they promised, he knew that there had to be ten times more at Tenochtitlán. He had not come this far to be turned back by promises. He could see that some of Moctezuma's nobles were not averse to trying to make their own deals. That didn't surprise him; it was a common enough practice with a long history where he came from.

The next day he reached Chalco, a city of twenty thousand, where he was presented with small gifts of gold and forty slave girls. In the morning, he was met by twelve Aztec lords who had come to give him greetings. The most important of them was another nephew of Moctezuma, Cacama, a young man of twenty-five who was carried in a litter on the shoulders of slaves. When he stepped down, the ground in front of him was swept away to remove any stones or objects that might hinder his progress. He gave greetings through Marina and told Cortes of their purpose. They were to escort the Spaniards the rest of the way to Mexico to ensure that there would be no trouble from recalcitrants in their path who had no love for the strangers.

From Chalco they moved to Culhuacan, where Cuitlahuac, its lord, made them welcome, opening his palaces to the Spaniards, who were much impressed by what they saw. The cities on the other side of the mountains had been rich, but these were the equal of the finest in Europe. The palaces were filled with gardens and pools, flower-covered lanes, groves of fruit trees, and animals and birds of many kinds that walked unafraid among them.

Here Cortes spent three days to rest his men and animals. They were close to their destination now, and he wanted his men to be at their best when they met Moctezuma. He didn't notice that a new arrival was in his ranks, marching with the foot soldiers, his face covered most of the time by a scarf. Casca had rejoined the Spaniards, but he didn't speak even to Juan, who passed him riding on his horse. From Juan's posture, Casca knew that the young man had given himself over completely to the ideology of the Castilian conquistadors. He turned his face away from his one-time friend. This was not the time for questions. Twice he had seen Marina. She'd spotted him easily but had said nothing. The ways of gods were not hers to question.

They could smell the lakes from Culhuacan, and from its temple in the distance they could make out easily the white structures on the island where Moctezuma resided. Cortes was led by Cacama to Ixtapalpa, which was connected with Mexico by means of another long causeway like the one Casca had taken from Chapultepec.

Marching in good order on the causeway, they came to a stone bastion between them and Tenochtitlán. It was two fathoms high, with towers at both ends between crenellated bastions. There, four thousand richly dressed gentlemen of the city waited to greet him. As Cortes neared, they each in turn bent over, touched the earth with a hand, and kissed it before moving on. Such was their manner of welcome. It took over an hour for the ceremony to be completed, and Cortes and his men waited impatiently for what came next. Past the battlement, they continued on the causeway. The waters on either side were bright and sparkling in the early sun. Before the causeway reached the main walls of Tenochtitlán, it was broken by a wooden drawbridge ten paces in length where the waters from one lake flowed into the other.

Suddenly Cortes saw what he had come to this place for. At the far end of the bridge stood Moctezuma under a pallium of green feathers strung with beads of silver. The pallium was carried by four men of noble blood to shield their lord from the elements. Moctezuma came forward. Macama and Cuitlahuac, both members of his family, supported each of his arms.

Cortes's first impression of the master of the Aztecs was of a dark, handsome man of great dignity and bearing, wearing golden sandals set with gems and a few articles of jewelry in the likeness of birds or beasts, made with incredible delicacy. Servants walked ahead of him, taking off their mantles and laying them down so that their master would not have to walk on the bare earth. Two hundred lords came next. Some of them Cortes had seen earlier. All were barefoot but dressed more richly than those who had greeted him first on the causeway. Moctezuma walked in the center of the street, and the rest of his retinue followed, hugging the walls and keeping their faces downcast so that they might not look directly into the face of their lord, for that would have shown irreverence.

Cortes dismounted from his horse and stepped forward by himself to greet Moctezuma. He started to embrace the king but stopped when Moctezuma withdrew as if a bit frightened. Gifts were exchanged. Cortes gave Moctezuma a necklace of cut glass, and Moctezuma presented Cortes with a necklace of gold, hung with finely worked images of shrimps an inch long, which he put around the neck of the conquistador with his own hands. It was an act which awed those of the Aztec party, for it was a sign of great favor and honor for the king to actually touch another man.

If those in the city had known of the way their king regarded the newcomers, they would have understood his manner of deference, but only a few of his closest advisers knew his secret—that these men were indeed the god in his many manifestations returning to claim the land. Not all with whom he had spoken agreed with him. To them the strangers were only that and no more. They were men with strange weapons and faces but certainly not gods, though the more superstitious called them such.

Together, Moctezuma and Cortes entered the city of Tenochtitlán passing tall houses on either side of the street. The roofs were covered with the people of the city, who gazed in amazement at the strangers with fair skin and hair, their beards, horses, and weapons of steel. Moctezuma led them a short distance to the courtyard of the house of Axayacatl, where the most sacred idols were kept for special festivals. At the door, Marina translated Moctezuma's words for Cortes to hear.

"Our lord, you are weary. The journey has tired you, but now you have arrived on the earth. You have come to your city, Mexico. You have come here to sit upon your throne, to rest under its canopy.

"The kings who have gone before have guarded it and preserved it for your coming. The kings Itzicoatl, Moctezuma the Elder, Axayacatl, Tizoc, and Ahuitzol ruled for you in the city of Mexico. The people were protected by their swords and sheltered by their shields.

"This was foretold by the kings who governed your city,

and now it has taken place. You have come back to us. You have come down from the sky. Rest now and take possession of your royal house. Welcome to your land, my lord!

"You are now in your house. Eat, rest, and enjoy yourself, and I shall return later."

Cortes responded through Marina, speaking loudly and firmly so that no one would hear the quiver of nervous excitement in his voice: "Tell the king that we are come as his friends. There is nothing to fear. We have wanted to see him for a long time, and now we have seen his face and heard his words, and it is good. Tell him that we love him and that our hearts are content to be in his presence."

Thus it was that Cortes had at last come to the city of Mexico and met with the king Moctezuma on November 8, 1519. He did not notice that as he spoke, Moctezuma's eyes often went to the commonly dressed soldier behind him, a soldier with a scarred face.

Casca found a place in the courtyard where he could keep some distance between himself and the other infantry men. It was well that he had kept his own counsel and company during the time he had been with the forces of Cortes. Because of that, he could lose himself among them and if questioned could always say that he was with another unit. His only regret was having to walk now, for he could not claim his horse without making his return known.

A request for Cortes to dine with the king that evening came shortly after the Spaniards had settled down. Even with the words of welcome, Cortes did not relax his vigilance. Guards were posted as they always were.

Cortes could hardly have imagined the emperors of ancient Rome dining in more majesty or being treated more regally. None of Moctezuma's people were permitted to sit in his presence or wear shoes or look him in the face, with the exception of a few great lords he was fond of or needed. Among the Spanish, only Cortes was given this privilege, and Cortes made it clear to his men that under no circumstances would they offend the customs of this king.

Moctezuma changed his clothes four times a day, never wearing the same outfit twice. His castoffs were given as presents to those who served him, and they were greatly prized for having been next to the skin of the king.

He was an unusually clean man, bathing twice a day, a thing which astonished most of the Spaniards, who thought too much bathing would wash away the protection that a good coat of grease and dirt gives the body. At a small, informal dinner such as the one Cortes attended, the dishes were served at one time by four hundred pages who were all the sons of nobles. Moctezuma would make his choices, indicating those he preferred, and the dishes would be set on braziers to keep them warm. Once he had made his selection for dinner, as many as fifteen or twenty of his most beautiful wives would enter to serve the dishes as he wanted them. There were several old men of good family who sat by the king's side and took morsels from his dishes and ate them with great reverence, never looking at his face. During the meal, clowns, hunchbacks, and dwarfs performed acrobatics for the king's pleasure.

When the meal was finished, what was not eaten was given to the warriors of his household guard. Each day, all three thousand of them were fed from the leftovers from the king's table. The plates were as fine as any potter in Spain could have made, and they too were never used for more than one meal. When the meal was formally finished and the table cleared, those he chose to talk or visit with would remain. The others would withdraw quietly. Only his servants, who stayed at the far end of the hall, where they could see if their master wished anything from them, were permitted to stay.

It was after this meal that Moctezuma spoke again to Cortes. Marina and Gerónimo kept their eyes averted from the face of the king. They were permitted in this place only as the servants of Cortes, and she was not given or offered food. They were there only to translate. Moctezuma wondered why this manifestation could not speak his tongue and the scarfaced one could. Another mystery.

Moctezuma spoke gravely and seriously with all the dignity of his office. Only the two kinsmen whom he trusted were permitted to hear his words. He knew that there were those who did not approve of his actions. To Cortes he bowed his head.

"My lord, I am pleased that you have come to my house at last. If I begged you not to come before, it was because my people were afraid of you and your wild beasts and because you have come from heaven and brought the thunder with you. I know that your warriors are mortal men and that you are the manifestation of he who was promised, as I said earlier. You know that with your coming there have been rebellions against me and that some of my vassals have become my foemen. But I will deal with them as they merit in time.

"Do you see that I am only a mortal man like any other and not a god, though I have to maintain my dignity for the sake of my high office? The houses you see are only common things made of sticks and mud, and there are few such as this poor place of stone. I tell you this so that you should know the truth of my possessions, which are now yours. Yes, we have some gold and silver that you value for some reason most highly, whereas for us the swords you wear are worth more than ten times their weight in gold or silver, for we do not have such metal in my land. But what gold and silver we have is also yours and will be brought to you when you wish it done. For as you and you alone know, we have met before, and as you said you would, you have come again."

These words confused Cortes somewhat. He could only believe that perhaps Marina and Gerónimo were not able to translate literally everything the king said. Still, if the king wished to think him a god or a god's aspect, who was he not to let him do so, for it would greatly simplify what he wished to do. He knew now that he could take all Mexico through the use of Moctezuma as his servant and vassal. Through the mouth of Moctezuma would go the words that would deliver to him the wealth, the land, and the people of this valley.

CHAPTER SEVENTEEN

As Moctezuma left Cortes, Casca moved behind him. Ignoring the Eagle knights of the king's escort, he spoke softly so that only Moctezuma could hear him. "We must meet tomorrow at my temple in the city. I shall be waiting for you at midday. Order the priests there to leave the temple and not return until you command it."

When the king left, the door was immediately secured by the Spaniards, a crossbowman and two arquebusiers placed in front of them with their ungainly matchlocks. Casca thought that the crossbows were more practical, had as much range, and were faster to load, but the muskets had a greater effect on the minds of the Indians. He wondered how long the fear of such weapons would last and when the Indians would stop believing them to be magical devices. In time, if they had time, they would lose much of their fear of the Spaniards and their weapons. Familiarity removes many fears, and once the Indians no longer saw the Castilians as nearly mystical beings, things would change rapidly.

In the morning, Moctezuma came to take Cortes on a tour of his city. The island had sixty thousand houses and a population of three hundred thousand. There were palaces, temples, streets and markets for vendors and merchants, and places where justice was given and punishments and rewards meted out.

With their escorts they went to the *teocalli* of the war god Huitzilopochtli and Texcatlipoca, his brother, the god of plenty and harvests. Each temple was like a small city of its own, served by specific villages who were responsible for its upkeep and the maintenance of its priests. Around the temples were altars and chapels used as sepulchers for the nobles as well as places of devotion and sacrifice. The temples were all placed so that the people who prayed to the rising sun would face them in their devotions.

Each entrance to the *teocallis* had large halls with connecting chambers on either side where arms and supplies were stored. Other chambers with small, dark doors held the images of the gods. Hundreds of idols, all of them black with human blood, were tended by the devout. Each idol had to be cared for. After a sacrifice, blood was collected and brought to these dark places, and each of the idols was washed in it. The cloying, sweet, sickening odor of death that was exuded from these chambers made more than one Spaniard feel the need to vomit from the purulent stench. It didn't seem to bother the priests at all, for they came every day to tend their masters and pray.

Moctezuma led the way up the terraces, each one smaller than the last, until they reached the top, over two hundred feet in height. At the top were two large altars set close to the edge of the platform. Their sides were painted with the different aspects of the gods and their minions. To the Spanish, all of them were horrible demons and devils. Most horrible of all were the huge idols of the gods Huitzilopochtli and Texcatlipoca, which were made of stone weighing several tons and stood over twice the size of a tall man. They were covered over in mother-of-pearl in which were set precious stones: emeralds, rubies, pearls, and topazes. Around their waists like belts were thick snakes of gold; on the neck, each wore a necklace of golden hummingbirds. There was a golden mask set on each head with polished eyes of obsidian, and at the backs of their heads, a dead man's face looked out.

Each altar had a small chapel of carved wood with three levels, one above the other. Seen from a distance, they looked like tall towers.

From there, Cortes and his escort, which included Juan,

who looked very proud at being granted the honor of attending his leader, had their first look over the city of Tenochtitlán. The waterways were crowded with boats, rafts, and canoes, bringing the things the city required: food, slaves, gold, and reeds from the marshes. Cortes sucked in his breath. Only now did he realize how much he had gambled for.

This was a greater city than Venice, more beautiful and richer, and it was being offered to him. If he wished, he could be king of this land and keep it for himself as his own domain. The thought was appealing, but he knew that it would not do. He was only the first of his race to come; soon there would be others. If he could gain the power he had over the Indians, others could do the same. It was difficult to push the thought of having his own kingdom away, but he knew that there was no choice. If he claimed these lands for himself rather than the king, it wouldn't be long before he would be assassinated by one of his own men.

Moctezuma told him of the priests and acolytes who served the god. At this one site, five thousand men were in constant attendance to serve the god's needs. Not even the Pope in Rome had such completely devoted servants in such numbers, for this was only one temple in a city of temples.

When they left the temple of the war god and his brother, they passed what resembled a theater built from the skulls of enemies taken in battle. The skulls were set so that they faced teeth outward. At the upper part of the theater were hundreds of tall poles, five spans apart, into which pegs had been driven, each of them holding five skulls impaled through the temples. Juan de Castro tried to count them one day and lost track at over a hundred thousand.

During the tour, the Spaniards said little, astonished by the magnificence of the city and the horror of its religion. Many rosaries were touched and silent Hail Marys said by the devout on their visit.

Moctezuma bade Cortes forgive him as he had duties yet to attend to. Then he left the Spaniard at his new house.

With a small guard of two hundred Eagle knights escorting his litter, Moctezuma went to the temple of the Quetza. It was round instead of a pyramid, for this temple was dedicated to the god in his aspect of the wind and air, for the air encompasses the sky. At the entrance, he left his escort behind with orders not to come in after him or disturb him. He had to speak to the god alone. His knights obeyed, watching the back of their king as he entered through a door carved like a serpent's head with the fangs extended.

The priests normally in attendance to the god were not to be seen, as he had ordered. The inside of the temple was decorated with painted frescoes and bas-relief carvings of the god Quetzalcoatl. Of all the gods of Mexico, he was the most peculiar, for he had more faces than any other and was the most complicated. The gods of war and harvests were easy to understand. The war god needed the hearts of warriors to feed him, and the lord of harvests required the blood of virgins to be spilled into the earth to renew the seasons. But the Quetza was different in all things. At the same time he was the god of learning, the god of the evening star, and the god of the air and the winds. He was the only one who had been given, by the wise men and shamans, a date on which he would return to the valley—1 Reed!

Moctezuma bowed low before the altar. A golden serpent with eyes of rubies curled around a disk representing the sky and heavens glowered at him. He lowered his eyes from the stones before the altar and waited.

"I am pleased that you have come. Rise and listen to me. We have things which must be said."

Moctezuma obeyed, lifting his eyes to see Casca seated on the lowermost golden coil of the serpent idol. Over his face was the jade mask, and on his shoulders, covering his breastplate of Spanish steel, was a cloak made with the tiny breast feathers of hummingbirds. The cloak had taken a master weaver three years to make, an iridescent work of art that breathed and moved with a life of its own with lights of blue and green interwoven and burning. Tens of thousands of tiny sparkles of light danced with the flickering of dozens of oil lamps set around the altar. Over his head, the figure of the golden serpent watched the king of the Aztecs with malevolent ruby eyes, its white fangs bared and ready to strike.

Casca had thought long about what he should say. The words were not easy or what he knew had to happen pleasant. To see this proud man kneeling before him, thinking him a god, was not something he relished, but there was no other way.

"Listen to me carefully. I know that you are confused and frightened by what is happening. Do not be. If Cortes does not seem to understand why you say certain things to him, do not worry, for he is only part of me and has no need to know certain things. But I hear and understand. That is all you need to know. A time of trial is coming for you and your people. Your world as you know it is going to end. You cannot save it."

Moctezuma sobbed out, "Do you mean that we shall all die?"

Casca shook his head, his eyes sad behind the stone mask. "Not all and perhaps not many. That is the mission I give you, to save the lives and much of the culture of your nation. From this day there is no going back. If your people resist the Spanish, then they will be destroyed utterly, never to rise again. Cortes and his warriors will make mistakes and will offend many by their manner; that is of no import. Keep those they offend under control, even to giving up your own life. I know that what I demand is not easy for you and that many of your nobles will not accept it without struggle. Some of them will try to kill the Spaniards. Do not let them succeed.

"If these ones who have come to your city are destroyed, then you will have no hope at all for the future of your nation, for others like them will come. As do locusts, they will ravage your land and take it for themselves, leaving your people only the ashes of memory to sustain them. And they will die not only from battles but from a sickness of the soul they will not be able to resist, and your nation shall be cast down."

Moctezuma wept openly, for all this had been predicted long ago. "I will obey, lord, but is there no other way? Cannot the other gods help us? Can they not save us? Speak to them for us. Ask them to aid us, for they are your brothers and will listen to you."

Casca had no good answer for the king. To say that there were no other gods would be to deny his own existence and divinity. Rising from the serpent's coil, he turned his back so that the king would not see the tears of his god running from beneath the jade mask.

"There is no help for you from anyone but me. This is a time of the dying, not only the dying of your nation but of your gods too. Our time has come to give ground for a new way, as nations give way to stronger lords."

Moctezuma came to his feet, hands extended and pleading. "Even you? Are you going to leave us?"

The god shook his head as he turned back around. "It is not that I shall leave you. You shall leave me, and this time there will be no returning for either of us. Now leave me and remember what I have said. The fate of your people is in your hands."

Moctezuma obeyed. He left the god alone in his temple, returning to his warriors, the stain of tears on his face bearing mute testimony to the depths of his despair. The Knights of the Eagles looked at each other, wondering what had taken place inside the temple. They knew from one of the priests who served the temple that only the king was inside. Yet they had heard more than one voice coming from it, though they couldn't make out the words. Perhaps their king had had a visitation from the Quetza.

Trouble was beginning. Cortes learned that nine of his men had been killed by Cualpopca, the governor of an Aztec province near the borders of Cempola. Pedro de Ircio had written to him of the deaths, saying that he had avenged them by destroying the Cualpopca's capital and by driving him and the Aztecs out of the city. Cortes blamed Moctezuma for this and when next Moctezuma came to him placed him under arrest, saying that it was for his own protection and to prove his devotion and friendship. There was very nearly a battle started by Moctezuma's Eagle knights when they saw this happen, but they were stopped by the king when he explained that he was not a captive, that he had decided to stay with the Spaniards as it was his pleasure to do so. This was not believed by all, but he was the king, and no one could do any more now than obey him.

Twice during the next week Moctezuma went to see Cortes, wondering what was going to happen next. The god had spoken, and he knew that what he had said was true. There very likely would be trouble from his nobles and subjects, but there was no way to do anything differently. The god had spoken, and this he related to Cortes as they walked through the gardens and menageries of his palace. To Cortes and the Spaniards, the gods Moctezuma spoke of were devils, and they placed no trust in the words of Moctezuma or any other. Even when Moctezuma tried to convince Cortes of his loyalty, he was not believed completely. Cortes demanded that he be given Cualpopca to stand trial, not before the Aztecs but before him.

This was done. Moctezuma's power was such that Cualpopca, along with his aides and officers, came to him voluntarily from a distance of sixty leagues. When he was questioned about his reason for attacking the Spaniards, he answered very honestly that he thought he was doing the will of the king, for he could not imagine his lord making such as them welcome. Cortes accused Moctezuma of treachery and had Cualpopca and fifteen of his nobles sentenced to death and burned in public before the people of Tenochtitlán, with Moctezuma standing beside him to let all know who was now the master of the Aztecs.

When the executions were over and the charred bodies had been removed by friends and family, Cortes again confronted Moctezuma with accusations, to which Moctezuma once more replied he was the best friend and ally the Spanish had. Cortes ordered him to prove the truth of his words by making a public proclamation to his nobles that he was now the willing vassal of the Spanish and that they were to likewise accept his rule over them.

Moctezuma agreed and sent forth his messengers to the great men of his empire. They were summoned to him from all corners of his lands to meet in grand council at his palace. Moctezuma dressed in regal splendor, his wand of office in his hand. Marina and Gerónimo were there to see that the king spoke as Cortes wished, and his Spaniards were present with weapons at hand ready for the first indication that some kind of trap was being set for them. They knew that on this island city they were very vulnerable, for they could be cut off and isolated.

Moctezuma played his part with a heavy heart, for even with the words of the god still in his ear, he did not like being the instrument of his world's collapse. To his nobles he gave these words:

"My kinsmen, friends, and servants, I have been your king for eighteen years. As my ancestors were before me, I have tried to be a good master as you have been my good and faithful friends and servants, and this I trust you are now and will be all the days of my life." At the words "my life," he recalled the words of the god who had said to him, *even to giving up your own life*! If he died, would his people still be loyal, and if so, to whom or what? He pulled his thoughts back to those who awaited his next words with fear and anger.

"You remember that which our fathers said, that we are not born of this country and our kingdom is not one to endure forever, because the rightful master of this land came from a distant land and returned there, saying one day that he would come back."

Casca stood behind a crossbowman as Moctezuma spoke. This part of the legend was not cited with the words he had used when he had left Teotihuacan, but after so many centuries, it was not unreasonable for stories to have items added or deleted. No matter, the tale would serve well enough.

Moctezuma leaned on the arm of his nephew Cacama as if the weight of his words were suddenly incredibly heavy.

"Those we have been expecting have returned. They are here before you." He indicated the hard-faced, pale Castilians.

"Let us give thanks to the gods that those we have so desired to see have come among us at last. You will please me by giving yourself and your loyalty to this man who is the representative and spirit of the god Quetzalcoatl. I implore you to obey him as you would me. Give to him all that you would give me, for all that I have is his. Swear him this service and you can do me no greater service or in a better fashion prove your love."

At his words the nobles wept openly. Groans and sobs came from their chests but they did as he commanded, for he was the king. But there were two who did not make the oath of fealty to Cortes, and only one man noticed. Casca saw clearly that while Cacama's mouth moved, no sound came out of it. The nephew of the king was looking straight at another man as he performed his mock oath. Cuahtemoc, a kinsman of Moctezuma as was Cacama, performed the same soundless ritual. Casca followed Cacama's eyes and knew that this was the beginning of trouble.

CHAPTER EIGHTEEN

Before Cortes had arrested Moctezuma, he had found a wall in his room where the whitewash was lighter in shade than it was on the other walls. He called in several of his men, and they scraped the wall clean and found a doorway that was now blocked with stone and mortar. Once this was cleared away, Cortes entered the room and found an amazing quantity of gold, artwork of silver and feathers, and idols and jewels beyond anything they had yet seen. As the hidden room was connected to his own quarters, he had the door resealed and said nothing of it to Moctezuma.

From the storehouses of the king, the Spaniards took everything that had belonged to Moctezuma, working themselves into a state of exhaustion as they ripped the gold trim from shields and ornaments and piled gold nose plugs and bracelets in heaps like so much trash. From the idols, they pried out the jewels and ripped off the necklaces of emeralds and turquoise. Even Juan was caught up in the madness, draping strands of precious stones around his neck and stuffing his purse with gold and silver. This was what he had come after! The Aztecs watched them in amazement, wondering why their gods did not strike the infidels down.

All this Cortes had removed to his quarters. If he had to

leave in a hurry, he would not leave with empty hands. There was enough in that one room to buy a hundred lifetimes of gracious living.

Cortes kept the chains of Moctezuma's confinement very loose. As long as he obeyed and made no trouble, he was allowed his own servants and was free to come and go as he wished without hindrance, except that there were always Spanish soldiers with his party. Cortes was confused by the way Moctezuma spoke to him. Sometimes it was as if Moctezuma thought he was a god; at others, as if he were a simple child who didn't know anything about the world he was living in. Much of Moctezuma's conversation had to be with his gods. For Cortes the defeat of the Aztec gods would be the next step to gaining complete control over the Indians. Making the religion of Spain their own would give him still greater control over the simple minds of the Indians.

This led to one of his few mistakes. In a moment of passion, when he and a party of his soldiers escorted Moctezuma to the temple of Huitzilopochtli, he had his men throw down the idols of the gods from their pedestals, smashing them when they could and striking those they couldn't break with their swords. The Eagle knights again had to be restrained by Moctezuma from attacking the Spaniards.

When Cortes saw the violent reaction of the Eagles, he thought it would be best not to pursue his efforts any further. If that was the manner in which all the Aztecs would respond to the destruction of their idols, it would be best to wait for another time. He did get Moctezuma to make one concession. There would be no more human offerings as long as the Spanish were in the city. Moctezuma agreed and gave the orders, but Cortes was certain that the priests were still making offerings of hearts and blood. However, he did not want to push the issue too far, for he was not yet in a strong enough position to enforce it.

From Mexico he sent out parties to scout the country and its peoples to find where the gold of the Aztecs came from and who their neighbors were. This was a time for consolidation, a time to build new friends among the tribes who were not subject to the Aztecs. If the Aztecs ever rebelled against him, they would be needed.

Casca had been right about Cacama. Within two months he

was in a state of near revolt from his city of Texcoco, where he was master. He had refused to admit the Spaniards to his city and drove them away with insults. When Cortes complained to Moctezuma of Cacama's attitude and treatment of his men, the king sent for his nephew, asking him to come to Tenochtitlán so that he might meet with Cortes in order to settle their differences peacefully. To this Cacama sent his answer by messenger!

"I feel no friendship for the Spaniards and less for their king across the sea, for they have taken away my honor and kingdom. There will be war, if not in your name then in mine, for the honor of our gods and fathers. I know that the words you send are not your own. They come from the mouth of the foreigner who stands with his knife at your back. I shall avenge you, too, my lord, and restore you to your proper place. The strangers have weakened your blood with words and lies, but I will not let them destroy our people or our gods. There shall be war!"

Cortes was worried and with good reason. Cacama had a reputation for being a tough man and had under his rule not only Texcoco but several other large cities. If he could gather on his side a few more Aztec lords with their forces, there was a good chance the Spaniards would never leave the land of the Aztecs alive.

Moctezuma knew what he had to do, for the god had warned him of this. He would stop his nephew, though it broke his heart to do so. He secretly called to him several lords and war chiefs who served with Cacama in Texcoco. Some obeyed him because he was still king, others because he promised them rewards of cities if they would serve him.

Cortes admired the manner in which Moctezuma dealt with the situation. The ability to suborn and connive was always among the attributes of a good leader. It was always better to use brains instead of weapons in the field, and in the long run it was much less expensive. Cacama was seized during a council meeting and brought in bonds to Tenochtitlán. Before bringing him to the king, his captors placed him in a gilded litter, as befitted his noble station. They carried him on their shoulders to face the judgment of the Spaniards through the mouth of their king.

For once Cortes listened to Moctezuma, who told him that

if they put Cacama to death or harmed him in any way, there
would be civil war, for then none of the great lords would feel
secure. They would band together against the Spaniards. This
made sense to Cortes. He gave orders that Cacama was not to
be harmed but was to be held with manacles to prevent his
escape. He would remain under the guard of Spanish soldiers
at all times.

In anticipation of trouble, Cortes increased his demands for
the Aztecs to bring him their treasures. The gold began to pile
up. Idols, statuary, plates, and goblets were melted down to
make their handling easier. Countless works of priceless art
went to the melting pots for the sake of convenience in handling. The treasures of the Aztecs were his, for the people were
used to obeying their kings without question, although some
of the Aztecs tried to keep their wealth for themselves. This
the Spaniards considered a very unreasonable and unfriendly
thing to do.

If it had not been for the number of his Indian allies, Cortes
was certain that he would have been attacked and killed. The
Aztecs did not like having their ancient enemies in their city or
mocking them at their borders.

To the enemies of the Aztecs, Cortes sent greetings and
gifts, planning against the day he was increasingly certain
would come. This worry was compounded when from Vera
Cruz he received word that one Panfilo de Narvaez, a friend
of his old enemy, Alvarez, the lieutenant governor, had come
against him. He brought with him eleven ships and an army of
men and arms for the sole purpose of destroying Cortes and
his men so that he could take the gold they had gathered for
themselves.

He would have to leave Tenochtitlán or lose his bases on the
coast. His anxiety was further increased when Moctezuma had
asked him several times in the last few days to leave Mexico
with all his men unless he wished to get himself and all of them
killed. For every day he was less certain of whom among his
lords he could count on. He promised Cortes that if he left for
a time, he would be able to regain his power and the Spaniards
could come back.

Cortes rejected Moctezuma's suggestion. He would not give
up what he had gained, but he still had to leave for the coast.
He gambled, though this was not a time when he would have

chosen to split his forces. He felt that he had no choice.

He left the care of the city and the king in the hands of Pedro de Alvarado, a pious Christian and a brave captain. Cortes took all his horses but ten and called in all his men who were out scouting the countryside. He left Pedro one hundred and fifty men and two cannon along with a thousand Tlax-calans and Cempolans to guard their captive king and their treasure; then he marched for the coast to deal with Narvaez.

Among those who remained behind were Juan de Castro and Casca. It was becoming increasingly difficult to avoid meeting with de Castro. Casca had to make special efforts to dodge his one-time friend. It was with regret that he saw the change in the young man—his contempt for the Indians and lust for the treasures of the Aztecs. Juan de Castro was ex-periencing the full arrogance of his pride and youth. Casca felt as if he had somehow failed him. If he had remained with Juan, perhaps he could have prevented his being infected by the madness that rode the rest of the conquistadors.

There were some who watched the Spanish force leave their city with satisfaction. Cuahtemoc stood on the pyramid of the fire god Xiuhtecuhtli with his bodyguard of Ocelot warriors. He prayed that the Spaniards would destroy themselves on the coast; then, in time, he would exterminate those few who re-mained in his city with their hated allies.

Cortes had been gone three weeks when a delegation of nobles petitioned Pedro for permission to hold the annual festival of the war god. Pedro had been ordered by Cortes not to do anything to cause trouble if it could be avoided, and he was curious about how the celebration was conducted. He gave them permission, stating only that there must be no human sacrifice.

Once the Aztecs had permission, they began to prepare for the celebration. The women began to grind the seeds of the chiclote in the patio of the temple under the eyes of the Castilians, who kept a careful watch on the preparations. From the seeds the women made a thick paste and from that began to construct a statue over a wicker frame, giving it the body of a living man in every detail.

When it was completed, they dressed it in the finest of feather work and painted crossbars of black over and under the eyes. Earrings of mosaic serpents worked in turquoise were

hung from its ears. A gold nose plug in the shape of an arrow
was set in place. On its head they set the magic headdress of
hummingbird feathers, and around its neck an ornament of
yellow parrot feathers trimmed with gems. Then came his cape
of nettles painted black, decorated with five clusters of eagle
feathers to symbolize Mexico.

Next came the cloak and vest, decorated with skulls and
bones, painted with pictures of dismembered human bodies,
skulls, ears, feet, hearts, hands, and intestines. In its left hand
they placed a shield, in the other four arrows. On its headdress
was set a sacrificial dagger made of red paper. The god was
ready for his people to pay homage.

Pedro de Alvarado, accompanied by de Castro, who felt as
he did, observed the preparations with a growing feeling of
disgust at the blasphemy of the savages and their loathsome
worship. His hands sweated freely as he tightened his grip on
the handle of his sword. The animals! They should all be
slaughtered so that this place would be cleansed of their vile
practices and made pure for the glory of the living Christ instead of these filthy blood-soaked idols.

Casca stood in the background, watching the Aztecs and the
Castilians. It was not good that Cortes was gone at this time.
He could see from the paleness of the lips on de Alvarado and
Juan that the men wanted to kill.

Cuahtemoc also watched the preparations. He knew what
the strangers felt for his people and their religion, but he was
not displeased at Cortes leaving one such as de Alvarado in
charge. He could see clearly that the Spaniard was a man of
great passion. Things were going to turn out as he wished.

When the sun rose the next morning, the statue's face was
uncovered by those chosen for that privilege. Gathering in
single file in front of their god, they offered it gifts of food.
The statue was not carried to the top of the temple; it would
remain in the patio until the dancing was over. The young warriors from both the Eagle knights and the Ocelots began the
dance. The Ocelots were there because their patron was the
brother of the war god.

Then began the dance of the serpent as the patio filled with
men who had fasted many days to purify their bodies and
spirits for the occasion. The dancers were kept in a single file
by those who fasted and were tapped with wands if they began
to lose their place.

The warriors danced without resting, hour after hour. If they had to urinate, they did so without leaving the line. Each of the warriors was dressed in his finest attire. The patio was a swarm of brilliant colors that weaved and bobbed to the beat of skin and clay drums, a rainbow serpent that twisted and leaped to the trill of flutes.

From the temple of the war god, Cuahtemoc rested one hip on the altar, pleased to see that he had been correct in his analysis of the Spaniards' reactions to the festival. Even now Castilians were moving in to block off the entrances to the patio, and de Alvarado, with de Castro, whom he had made his aide de camp, escorted by ten of his men, was walking toward the altar in front of the idol where the offerings of food had been made. This was what Cuahtemoc had been waiting for.

Casca was with the detachment of Spaniards securing the southern entrance to the patio. He could see de Alvarado as he stood in front of the statue of the god and looked down at the offerings which had been brought to it. The scream of rage and fury bursting out of the throat of the Spaniard grated over the high trillings of the flutes. There, among the cakes and flowers, he saw the dismembered body of a baby set out delicately as food for the god.

Crying out to his men, he drew his sword and began to slash at the dancing figures, cutting them down. Joined by de Castro and his escort, they began to slaughter the unarmed dancers. From the Spaniards, who now surrounded the patio, came the crack of musket fire. Then they moved in with sword and pike, wading into the dancers, killing everyone they could reach. Juan de Castro attacked the man playing the largest drum and cut his arms off at the shoulders. Then, with a full swing, he separated his head from its body.

The Spaniards went into a blood frenzy. They killed everyone within their reach, slicing bellies open with their steel swords, letting the intestines fall to the ground, where their owners tripped over them as they tried to flee. There was no escape, and that was what Cuahtemoc wanted. He needed a reason to go to war that none of his people could deny. This was it.

The blood from the dead flowed into pools that covered the stones of the patio as de Alvarado cried out to his soldiers, "They want blood and death to satisfy their gods; then we shall give it to them in full measure.'' No one escaped. Every dancer was butchered, and the stench of death drifted over the city as it had never done before. Juan stood with arms too heavy to raise anymore, his feet splayed out to balance himself. His chest and sides heaved with the exertion of the slaughter. He was numbed and exhilarated by the good work he had done this day for Christ, Castile, and Cortes.

Cuahtemoc had his war, and no one could stop it now, not even Moctezuma. The Spaniards would pay, and he would have their bodies on the altars.

CHAPTER NINETEEN

Cuahtemoc sent forth his messengers throughout the city. They cried out, "The strangers are killing the dancers. Hurry, bring your shields and your spears." The people of the city let loose a great groan, for the dance was a thing sacred to the gods. For the strangers to attack the unarmed warriors in the patio of the temple was too great a horror to endure. Their frustrations had reached the breaking point. From all over the city they came. They raced over the causeways connecting Tenochtitlán to its tributary cities. Canoes filled with men swarmed onto the waters of the lake. The warriors came crying out for vengeance.

Pedro de Alvarado stood in the center of the patio, his boots soaked in blood, the bodies of the dancers lying about him. His hands trembled with his passion. He knew that he had done the right thing in the eyes of God. From the wall encircling the courtyard he heard a cry of "*Madre de Dios*." One of his men fell onto the stones, an Aztec spear protruding from the side of his face. From the other Spaniards on the wall, he heard the cry, "In the name of God, run. They are coming. The Aztecs are coming!"

The Spaniard quickly regained control of his passion, calling his men to him. With Juan de Castro on his right, he formed a square and began moving back. A cloud of arrows swept over them as they protected themselves beneath their shields. Spears followed as warriors of the Eagles, Ocelots, and Coyotes threw themselves at the Spaniards, dragging several of them down. If it had not been for their armor and steel weapons, they all would have been taken.

Reaching a narrow, high-walled corridor where the Aztecs had to come at them on a narrow front, they fought their way back to the palace. Several more of their men fell, although most were only wounded. They had to be left behind; there was no time to stop and render aid. If a man fell, the Aztecs had him, and there was no help from his comrades.

De Alvarado wept as he saw the fallen Castilians being carried over the heads of the Aztec warriors and passed from hand to hand. He had been in this savage land long enough to know what was going to happen to them.

An Ocelot knight hurled his body over the heads of the rear rank of Spaniards, his flint-lined *macama* slicing off the lower jaw of a crossbowman. Casca caught him as he fell, grabbing the man's wrist and breaking it before he ran his sword into the knight's throat. Once more the Aztec custom of taking prisoners rather than just killing their enemies made possible the escape of de Alvarado and his men. Of the hundred he had brought to the dance, twenty were wounded and six did not make it back to the palace.

As soon as they reached the doors of the palace, they began to barricade them. The cannon were loaded, set with ball and grape, and for the first time since they had been in the city, fired. Each round killed twenty to thirty of the closely packed, howling warriors. But the losses in the Aztec ranks were quickly replaced by reinforcements rushing in from the outskirts of the city, eager to join in and savor the death of those who had humiliated their king and desecrated their holy places and gods.

Casca knew that this was the beginning of the end for the Aztecs. They might destroy the Spanish in the city, but they could not resist the future, which was going to roll over them in waves of blood and fire.

The palace of the king was well built of massive carved stone and had been designed for defense, which now served the Spaniards. Moctezuma sent his noble lord Itzcuauhtzin to speak to his people from the roof of the palace. The elderly statesman called out to the angry mass below:

"Aztecs! Your king has sent me to speak for him. Hear me, for these are his words to you. You must not fight the Spaniards, for we are not their equals in battle. Our people will suffer more greatly than you can imagine. Go back to your homes and return your captives. If you do not stop, then our nation shall perish. These are the words of the king who has spoken to me."

When Itzcuauhtzin finished, there was silence for a long moment. Then a low murmur began among the throng, building to a cry of rage as a noble of the Eagle knights from Moctezuma's own guard cried out, "We listen no more to Moctezuma. He is the slave of the Spanish and not responsible for what he says or does. Death to the Spanish and all traitors." A flight of arrows drove Itzcuauhtzin from the roof of the palace as his Spanish escort protected him behind their shields.

Behind him, out of view of the mob, Moctezuma had been listening. An arrow fell, ripping through his cloak. Moctezuma wept for his nation and his lost honor. For the first time he had heard them say that he was not their master any longer, and they had disobeyed his will in public.

De Alvarado was furious that Moctezuma had not been able to make his people stop their attacks. He quickly put the king in irons. There was no longer any doubt in anyone's mind about the status of the king of the Aztecs.

They couldn't get out, and the Aztecs couldn't get in. For seven days the warriors attacked around the clock. Their own numbers limited their movements, making them easy targets for the cannon now loaded with grapeshot. Each blast from the muzzle ripped the unprotected bodies of the Aztecs to shreds. Tearing limbs from their sockets, the grapeshot was a smoking scythe that harvested men.

The supplies from outside stopped. The bridges and passages connecting the palace to the rest of the city were cut. Canoes patrolled the walls nearest the lake. Anyone caught with food near the vicinity of the palace was put to death. The servants of Moctezuma, identified by their glass lip plugs, were killed on the spot. They would allow no one who might still be loyal to Moctezuma near the palace. Hundreds of their own people were killed for no more than vague suspicions. Any who had shown too much friendliness to the Spaniards were suspect. Cuahtemoc purged the city of all unwanted influences. If a few hundred died who were innocent of wrongdoing, it didn't matter, as long as he was able to keep the Spaniards bottled up without food or water.

For thirty days the small garrison of Spaniards and their royal hostages held the palace. Wells had been dug in the courtyard for water, and their horses fed on the plants of the gardens. They had no information from the outside world. What had happened to Cortes? Had he won his contest with Narvaez? Would relief be coming? Every day their supplies and munitions were depleted further. The furnishings of the rooms of the palace had been stripped of everything that could be used. The wood from benches, tables, and staircases had been cut down into arrows and bolts for their crossbows. Pottery and household artifacts of clay or brass were broken to make shot for the cannon.

Casca stood by a window, watching the streets below. His armor bore numerous hacks and gouges to testify to the violence of the siege. Below him he could easily see the Aztecs in their brilliant war costumes being exhorted to greater efforts by their captains. A figure moved beside him to look over his shoulder.

"They're terrible-looking devils, aren't they. Thank God for our good Spanish armor or they'd have all of us stretched out on their altars." Casca turned toward the voice. Juan froze when he saw the familiar scarred face looking at him.

"Carlos! I thought you were long dead. Where have you been?"

Casca removed his casque and ran fingers through his sandy hair, which was sticky with sweat and grime. "I've been around. As to exactly where I've been, that is not important." Reaching out a hand, he touched a necklace of emeralds and gold hanging around Juan's neck. "I see you've found that which you came for."

Juan detected a note of disappointment in the voice. "Yes, I have gathered enough of what I need to restore my family's fortune and make them a great name in Spain."

Casca shook his head sadly. "A great name. Is that all that you can see here?"

Juan didn't know what Casca meant. "What else is there to see except for the savages outside? When Cortes returns, we shall treat them as the animals deserve." His voice took on a touch of righteous fervor. "All that they have is ours by right of conquest and our duty to God. We shall bring them to Christ on the points of swords and make them our servants. This is our destiny!"

Casca turned his back to Juan. "I'm too late. You are the same as the others. I just hope that you are able to get back to Spain. Those gentlemen out there may have other plans, and you and all of these brave men may become a part of their destiny. Now go away from me, Juan. We have nothing more to speak of. Go back to your friends and your gold."

Juan felt a bit hurt and confused by Casca's reaction. He couldn't understand why his friend had spoken to him so. Well, if that was the way he wanted it, then good enough, that was the way it would be. He was not the same man who had been on board the caravel of Captain Ortiz. He was a full member of the company of Cortes and had proved his valor in battle. He would take Casca's advice and return to those who understood him and leave the dour and gloomy fellow to his own devices. He would do his duty and hold this place until the return of Cortes. By Saint James, he was a Castilian and would conduct himself as one.

On the thirty-second day of the siege, they heard cannon fire in the distance. Like magic, the Aztecs melted away, leaving the road open for the return of Cortes. This was done at the orders of Cuahtemoc. He had not wanted to kill all those in the palace. They served a greater purpose by being left alive and confined. Their leader would have to come back for them, and then he would have the Spaniards all in one spot with no way out.

Casca watched from the roof as Cortes rode into the city, breaking through the rubble of the barricades that had been built to contain the Spaniards in the palace. He had more soldiers with him than he had had when he left. His Indian allies were the Tlaxcalans, who had come back in force to punish their hated enemies. The warriors of Cempola had been left behind on the coast.

As Cortes entered through the city, there was a heavy silence over the once-bustling streets. Not a sound came from any of the buildings. He suspected an ambush, but there was no sign of any Aztecs on the roofs or hiding anywhere near his route of march. They had pulled back. Was it because they feared him and his reinforced army? He had defeated Narvaez and had added the survivors to his own army, along with another fifty horses.

All the way to the palace of Moctezuma he saw and heard nothing. His men were roundly cheered by the holdouts who thought they were being rescued. As soon as Cortes and his men and animals were inside the palace, the Aztecs renewed the attack, throwing up fresh barricades. They threw barrages of darts, arrows, spears, and stones at every opening from which the Spanish inside could shoot.

Cuahtemoc was jubilant; he had them all! Now, like snails in a cooking pot, it was time to build the fires to pull them out of their shells.

Cortes was furious at what had happened in his absence. Quickly, efficiently, he made an analysis of their situation. He inspected every room in the palace and placed his men where they could do the most good. An inventory of the weapons and supplies was disappointing. If they stayed under siege very long, they would starve.

What Casca had feared was coming true. The Aztecs knew that the Spaniards were only mortals and that their weapons were not magic. Familiarity had bred contempt and death. The myth of Spanish invincibility had been broken.

Cuahtemoc had shown his people the mortality of the Castilians on the altar of the war god. The captives taken by them were spread-eagled on the stones, weeping and crying for mercy. Only one went to the altar defiant and full of courage. He was given the greatest honor of any of the victims by being made the main course in a meal for the Eagle knights. His flesh was eaten but not savored. The flesh of the Spanish was not to the taste of the Aztecs. They would have preferred a nice fat dog to the meat of their enemies.

Once Cortes was convinced of the reality of his situation, he attempted to make the Aztecs fear the Spanish once more. He ordered an assault with two hundred of his Castilians and three hundred of his Tlaxcalan warriors. He broke his force into two parts, hoping to catch the bulk of the besiegers be-tween them, where his better armed men could butcher them with relative ease. In spite of de Alvarado's mistakes, Cortes had the feeling that this day would have come no matter who he had left in charge, and de Alvarado was still too good a captain not to be used. He was given command of one of the raiding parties.

At his signal, they both broke out of different sides of the palace, attempting to sweep into the center, forcing and bunching the Aztecs between them. The Aztecs had learned their lesson. They broke away, climbing to the roofs of the buildings and hurling stones down on the enemy, making the invaders fight man to man for every house. If the Castilians took a house, the Aztecs would set it on fire, forcing the Spanish back out into the open, where they could be properly brained.

Cortes was forced back into the palace, pursued by the Aztecs. They howled and screamed for the invaders' blood. If it hadn't been for the cannon, falconets, and arquebuses, they would have forced their way inside. As it was, the bodies of the dead and wounded Aztecs piled up in the entrance, providing a barrier of bodies from which the Spaniards could load and fire.

Once inside, they did a body count. Four were missing, three were dead, and eighty were wounded. Most of the serious wounds came from being hit in the head by falling rocks and bricks. Juan was one of the wounded. A stone from a sling had smashed the bridge of his nose, knocking him unconscious. He didn't know that the man who picked him up and carried him over a shoulder as he fought his way back to the palace had a scar running from eye to mouth.

Cortes tried again the next day, destroying a few houses and capturing a couple of bridges which he later had to relinquish. The losses of the Aztecs were ten times those of the Spaniards, but the Aztec ranks were constantly replaced with volunteers. When the Spanish lost a man to death, capture, or wounds, he could not be replaced. With each loss, their strength was sapped from them.

Casca was put to work building three wooden siege machines. Cortes hoped they'd enable him to get close enough to the surrounding houses to be able to destroy the Aztecs and clear them away from the palace. This would give his marksmen the advantage of range with which to use their weapons and would force the Aztecs to cross an open area to reach them.

While they were building the machines, Cortes went to Moctezuma, promising him his freedom if he would speak to his people again and persuade them to lift the siege and let the Spanish leave the city.

Casca was working on one of the machines in the palace courtyard when Moctezuma was brought from his quarters. The king of the Aztecs paused briefly when his eyes met those of Casca. He shook his head sadly as if to say, "I have done my best," and then was hauled off by his guard toward the battlements where he once more would try to stop the attack.

When he appeared on the battlements, the fighting ceased. A silence ran through the thousands of watchers. Cuahtemoc moved to the front in full battle dress. He wore the helmet of an Eagle knight and a shield rimmed with gold and trimmed with eagle feathers. He held his *macama* above his head to complete the silence. He had loved his king and admired him. Moctezuma was the last of his line and had been the best of them.

Moctezuma raised his arms above his head to speak, but at a command from Cauhtemoc, he was shouted down. Cuahtemoc could not take the chance that Moctezuma's words might, even at this point, influence his·warriors. Regretfully, he gave an order to his ten best slingers to let loose their stones. He did not want to kill Moctezuma, just keep him from speaking or interfering. The stones left their slings, and one found its mark on the king's temple. The sound of bone cracking was heard clearly by the now silent warriors. Moctezuma fell to the walkway of the battlements, where he was picked up and carried back to his rooms by his captors.

CHAPTER TWENTY

Moctezuma was nearly in a coma. Blood-tinged fluid came from his nose and ears. His nobles and family were in constant attendance. In his sleep he would call to the gods to witness that he had done his best for his people and ask the Quetzalcoatl to forgive him for failing them.

Cortes was enraged that the Aztecs could assault their own king. He liked Moctezuma as a man and a noble. It would be a great loss for the Spaniards should he die. Even with the city in revolt, there were many others of the Aztec nation who would rally to their king—if they were able to get out of Tenochtitlán alive to even ask them.

Casca wiped the blood from his sword. They had just beaten off another attempt by the Ocelot warriors to break through a section of the palace built of bricks and mortar. He pretended not to notice, as did the other Castilians, that the bodies of the dead Aztecs were not thrown outside as they had been in the past. Their Indian allies, the Tlaxcalans, took the dead with them to the part of the palace grounds where they camped. There was a kind of logic to this. If the Tlaxcalans sustained their strength on the flesh of the Aztecs, there would be more grain for the Spaniards to eat.

It wasn't difficult for Casca to lose himself in the midst of

the soldiers. With the reinforcements Cortes had brought with
him and the current state of siege, no one paid him any attention other than to call on him if his sword was needed. Juan
had recovered from his wound with little more than a nose
that would be slightly out of kilter for the rest of his life and a
headache that lasted for two days. He was told of his being
rescued by a scarred, stocky man who fought like a maniac as
he carried Juan on his shoulder. He had started to tell Cortes
about the return of Carlos Romano but, for some reason he
couldn't fathom, chose not to. If his friend, and he still
thought of Casca that way, wanted to keep a secret, he would
not say anything. He might not understand Romano, but he
did know that he was no traitor, nor was he a man without
honor.

Casca was concerned about the health of the king. From
what he had been able to find out, Moctezuma was fading
rapidly. He would not last many more days. The servants who
took food to his chambers, only to bring back full trays, said
that he called out many times for the god Quetzalcoatl to come
to him.

He waited for the second hour before dawn, when men's
souls were the deepest in sleep and the senses of those yet
awake were dulled. It had been three days since the stones of
the slingers had been thrown. He had to see the king before he
died.

Two Spanish sentries were on guard at the king's door.
Tired and hungry, they were near to sleep. Even while they
leaned against the stone walls, Casca walked easily up to them
in full armor, his face lost in the shadows of his helmet and the
dim light of the single torch near the doorway. In his hand he
held a flask of wine. It had cost ten gold pieces to liberate it
from one of the former soldiers of Narvaez. There was not
much of the precious fluid left, nor had there been for several
weeks. From the coffers in the basement of the palace, he had
found what he needed: leaves of the coca plant like those he
had used to dull his senses during the long walk to the altars of
Teotihuacan. The wine would be bitter, but it would give the
weary sentries rest.

He greeted the soldiers with a slight slur to his words, giving
the impression that he had already been at work on the flask.
"*Hola*, caballeros! The night is long, and the day promises

nothing to look forward to." He shook the flask. The gurgle of the bottle brought the guards' eyes to full awareness. Raising it, he pretended to drink. Sighing as if he were as tired as they, he leaned against the wall. Then, as if he had just noticed their stares at the wine, he apologized to them for his discourtesy, saying, "Enough of this. I am tired and have no taste for anything anymore. Here!" He tossed the flask to the taller of the guards and turned back the way he had come. Stopping at the staircase leading down to where it was dark, he waited.

The guards looked at the bottle and licked their lips. If they were found drunk on duty, it would go hard with them, but they were both grown men, and one flask of wine couldn't have much effect on such as they. There was no chance of its getting them intoxicated.

Casca was getting a little impatient, but at last he heard the gurgling of the bottle and knew that the guards were drinking. One of them gave a curse as he finished his swallow. "*Madre de Dios!* This is nearly as bitter as that vile concoction the Indians drink." His compadre laughed and tilted the lip of the flask to his mouth. Letting the muscles of his throat relax, he took half the contents in one swallow. His friend grabbed it back from the greedy lips and sucked down the rest of it, emptying the container. In the dark Casca gave a small grin. The wine might be bitter, but it was still wine. Now to wait a few minutes more. He rested his jaw on his forearms as the minutes passed. He couldn't see them from his position, but he could hear them clearly when the first blubbery snores drifted down the dark hallway. He waited to see if there would be any protest from the other guard. There was nothing, and he figured that the other man just didn't snore. He rose quietly, staying close to the wall until he could see the guards. They had both suddenly become very tired and were leaning back against the wall to support their strangely weak legs. They slid down to a sitting position as the essence from the coca leaves did its duty. They were out cold and would be for some time.

Opening the outside bolt to the carved door, Casca slid inside. Beside the king's bed sat Itzcuauhtzin, his eyes closed. The faithful retainer. Casca did not disturb his sleep. A small tap in back of the ear put the old noble into a deeper slumber.

The king moaned softly as Casca leaned over him and whispered, "I am here. I have come to you."

Moctezuma opened his eyes slowly. The lids were sticky with sickness. From the glow of the night outside his window, he could barely make out the face of Casca.

"My lord, you have come." He coughed, his face pale and wan. There was little strength left in him. Death would come for him before the next day saw the sun fall. Casca knew this. He had seen thousands die in every manner, and the cast of death on a man's face was something he knew better than anyone else.

He held the king's limp hand in his own, speaking gently. "Yes, I have come to you. Fear not, for you have done the best you could, but the stars have ordained otherwise. What must be will be."

Moctezuma tried to rise to his elbows but failed, falling back heavily to his pillow. His breath came in short gasps as he searched for the strength to speak.

"My lord god, what is to become of my people and of me?"

Casca gave the king's hand a gentle squeeze. "Your people are beyond anyone's help now. They must live with the future they have made. But you will be remembered and loved for the memory for as long as I exist."

Moctezuma smiled. "Then I will not go to my death unwilling. Yet there is one thing I would ask of you if I have served you well, my lord."

Casca tried to read the face of the king but couldn't. "What is it that I can do for you at this time, noble king?"

Moctezuma drew in a deep breath. "My lord, I would not die by the hands of my own people. Will you not accept me as an offering for them? Take me with your own hands that my death will not be the shame of my nation."

The request was totally unexpected, but Casca understood the reason for it. The greatest honor the king could have in these last minutes of his life, a life spent in dedication to his gods, would be to be taken by a god, a god who would take the king as a final offering for his people. Rising to his feet, he placed both his hands on the clammy face of the king. "I understand, Moctezuma, last king of Aztecs. I accept you as an offering. You have not sinned but have been a good and faithful servant to your gods and duty."

His hands slid down to the king's neck. "I take you now. Know that you are well loved, Moctezuma the king."

At peace, Moctezuma closed his eyes. He raised his chin so that the god's fingers could be placed easily on his throat.

Casca had killed many with his hands. He knew where to place the pressure so that there would be no pain, only a dullness that would turn into eternal sleep. He squeezed gently until the spirit of the last king left its earthly shell to join those of the others of his line. Moctezuma died feeling that he had been blessed and forgiven. His last thought, just before the darkness claimed him, was of the figure before him. When he opened his eyes for one last look at the Quetza, he wondered why the scar-faced god was crying.

CHAPTER TWENTY-ONE

From the rooftop, Cortes had Marina call out to the Aztecs for a truce, during which time the body of Moctezuma would be turned over to his people. This was granted, and Moctezuma was carried by members of his own family to be delivered. He was taken to Chapultepec for funeral rites amid great wailing and mourning. The Aztecs claimed that the Spaniards had killed their king, and the Spaniards said that it was the stone thrown by them that had caused his death. Only one man knew that both accusations were correct.

There were several minor forays by Cortes during the next few days, but any gains he made had to be given up quickly. He just did not have the strength to take and hold a city this size with its entire population in arms against them. There was only one thing to be done. They would have to try to get free of the city and back into the open. On the seventh day after his arrival, he was ready. His men had worked all that night making a portable bridge with which they hoped to be able to cross the canals whose bridges had been destroyed by the Aztecs.

During the last attack, he had lost two horses, and several of his men had been killed. He had been wounded in the arm and knee, but not badly enough to keep him from moving. However, it gave the Aztecs further proof of the vulnerability of the Spaniards and showed everyone once and for all that Cortes was only a mortal man.

Cortes gave the order to open the storerooms of Moctezuma where the treasures were kept.

The king's royal fifth was set aside in the presence of his alcaldes and regidores. He assigned them men and horses to transport the king's share. This way, if anything happened to it, he would not be held to blame. As for the rest of the treasure, which had been estimated to be over seven hundred thousand ducats worth, he told his men to take what they wanted. He was making them a present of it.

Those who had been with him from the first knew more of what they had to face. They took mostly jewels, stuffing their pockets with rubies, emeralds, and sapphires. Narvaez's men went for the gold and silver, weighing themselves down like pack animals in their greed.

As he watched the men of Narvaez load themselves with heavy gold and silver objects, Casca shook his head. They were going to pay dearly for every extra ounce they carried. Juan had his own treasure trove. Around his neck hung jewels on heavy chains of gold. In a sack he had something that he could not bear to leave behind. It was a gold sun disk set with rubies and emeralds weighing thirty pounds. Casca didn't try to persuade Juan to leave it behind. He'd seen the look on his friend's face and knew that it would be a futile effort. He wondered if the wound Juan received was still having some effect on him. In the last couple of days Juan had not looked well. There was fever in the eyes and a sweaty face that bothered Casca. Perhaps Juan's madness for gold came from a touch of fever.

He took only a pouch full of gems for himself. He had not come to this land for treasure, but he would need money to get him to the next place.

Casca was in the lead element when Cortes gave them the word for the breakout. It came at the stroke of midnight through a hole they made in one of the garden walls. Behind the lead element came forty men, carrying the portable bridge they would need to get over the canals and causeways that had been cut. Behind the bridge came the Tlaxcalans, carrying the cannon and supplies. Bringing up the rear were the prisoners who had been taken captive at the time they had arrested

Moctezuma. Most were members of his household staff, with several nobles among them. Cacama was one of them. Cortes thought they might yet prove to be useful when he made his return to Tenochtitlán.

Luck was with them for the first minutes. They were able to get over the first three canals without a problem, until they reached the Toluca causeway. The portable bridge had just been laid down, when a horse whinnied. From all around the road came cries of, "Brothers, it is the Spanish. They are escaping. Come, brothers, gather your spears and arrows!"

The Aztecs poured out of their houses, jumped from rooftops, and ran out of orchards as they raced for the escaping enemy. Boatloads of archers took to the water. The Castilians were hit from the sides and rear most heavily. The soldiers in the rear had to destroy their own bridge so that the Aztecs could not cross after them. As they withdrew from the city, they were hounded with war cries and arrows. The canoes kept pace with the column, letting loose hundreds of arrows, ignoring the return fire of the Spaniards.

The full brunt of the Aztec attack hit as they reached the Toltec causeway. Thousands of warriors hurled themselves at the hated enemy. Flint-lined *macamas* and spears searched out openings in Spanish armor as the Castilians were held to the ground. At a break in the causeway where a bridge had been destroyed, hundreds died as they tried to leap the expanse from one side to the other. The weight of the treasure they carried pulled them down. Horses and men clogged the gap, drowning or having their bellies slit open by Aztec swimmers. Their bodies formed a bridge over which their comrades raced. It was every man for himself. Pleas for help were ignored. From the mass of bodies, hands would extend into the air holding one of the items of gold they had stolen, offering it to anyone who would stop a second and pull them back up. There were no takers. Gold was not worth very much now. Others, more wise, dropped their loot to make better time.

Nearly all the treasures of Moctezuma were lost that night as the baggage animals went down, their sides filled with arrows or spears. Pedro de Alvarado stayed with the rear guard, trying to hold off the Aztec waves and rescue who and what he could. At last he saw that he could hold no longer, and the thought of being taken alive gave him a new strength. He was the last to make it across the canal, using his spear as a lever with which to launch his body over the gap. All those still behind him fell to the Aztecs, who screamed in pleasure as they pulled the Spaniards and Tlaxcalans down. These they would take alive for the gods.

All the women of the Tlaxcalans were taken as captives or killed. Only a few with Spanish lovers near the head of the column made it to dry land. Marina wept as she saw the defeat of the Spaniards by her ancient enemies. She passed Casca and stopped for a moment, her eyes pleading with the god to do something. Her hands began to rise in supplication and then dropped back to her sides as Casca wearily shook his head from side to side.

Casca heard voices crying out to them, pleading for help, but there was none to be given. He was still in the lead element when they reached the banks of the lake and were at last off that terrible highway of death. He cleared a space with his sword, cutting down four painted and feathered warriors of the Eagles to make room for those behind him. He expanded their bridgehead, which rapidly widened and gained strength as more Spaniards and Tlaxcalans reached the shore, from which they could at last fight on a broad front. Casca looked over his shoulder back toward the direction from which they had come. All over Tenochtitlán fires were lit on the temples. He knew what they were for. Tonight the ancient gods of the Aztecs would be sated with the blood of the conquistadors.

The Aztecs were in a solid mass, pushing at the rear of the Spaniards. Men were being trampled on and crushed to death under the feet of friends and enemies alike. Casca heard a voice above the throng crying out to Saint James. Juan! He moved back toward the way he had come. Shoving men out of his path, he tried to reach the voice. The last of the Spaniards were coming across with them. At last he saw Juan, his face bloody and his armor torn. The jewels around his neck had turned from green to red with his blood. He fought like a berserker, cutting and slashing at the brown hands trying to drag him down. No one helped. It was every man for himself. Hanging from Juan's shoulder by a wide strap was the sack in which he carried the sun disk. A slash from a razor-edged *macama* cut through the strap. The golden disk fell out to lie on the stones in a puddle of blood. Juan was only twenty feet away from the safety of the rear guard when the disk fell. He was almost there.

Juan slashed off the face of an Ocelot knight and started to make a final effort to reach the Spanish line. Facing the Aztecs with three others, he fought his way back five feet and then saw the disk under the feet of the Indians. The gold gleamed in the light of the fires; the jewels mocked him. He couldn't leave it. He left the three soldiers and ran toward the object. He would have the disk.

Casca cried out to him, "Leave it! Come back!" Juan didn't hear, and if he had, it wouldn't have changed his mind. He had to have the disk; it was his future for himself and his family. The other three men made it into the safety of the Spanish line. The Aztecs swarmed around Juan, pushing right up to the Spanish defense in a solid body. Casca couldn't get through to him. The last thing he saw was Juan being carried overhead by dozens of hands. They passed him from one band of warriors to another, taking him farther away. In his hand Juan held the gold sun disk. Then he was gone. Tears ran down Casca's face. He knew the fate waiting for Juan and only hoped that somehow he would be able to make the Aztecs kill him quickly. Another rush by the Aztecs took him back to the business of killing.

Across the canal, standing with knights of the Eagles and Ocelots and looking in his direction, was Cuahtemoc, wearing the priestly costume of Itzli, god of the obsidian knife. He wore the flayed skin of a noble warrior, human skin that was stretched and treated until it was as easy to wear as a tunic. From the skin of the flayed warrior the hands still dangled at the wrists and the face was stretched to fit over that of Cuahtemoc, who watched the retreat and death of the Spaniards through the eye sockets of a dead man's face. He was content.

Cortes led the way to Tacuba, where they had to fight another small battle. If the Aztecs had come after them in strength, they would have all perished. But the Aztecs, for some reason which the Spanish could not fathom, decided to wait. Casca knew that it was a mistake the Aztecs would pay for dearly.

They had left Tacuba and were on the road leading to Tlax-cala, where they would have friends and help. Many in the ragged column were moaning over the wealth they had left behind and were swearing that they wouldn't rest until they had the gold of Moctezuma once more in their grasp.

Cuahtemoc made this impossible. From the canals and waters of the lake, divers brought up the treasure. The bodies of the Spaniards and Tlaxcalans were stripped so that there would be nothing on them when they met the gods.

CHAPTER TWENTY-TWO

Four hundred and fifty Spaniards, forty-six horses, and over three thousand Tlaxcalans died in the few minutes from the time when they left the palace of Moctezuma to the time when they reached Tacuba. For the Spaniards, that time would be forever known as *la noche de tristes*, or the night of sorrows.

For others the night of sorrows was not over. In the city of the fishermen they made sacrifices of ten Spaniards by placing them in nets and then twisting and tightening until each victim's flesh and intestines were squeezed out of the mesh. This process took over two hours to complete.

At the altar of the war god, Cuahtemoc was ready to pay homage to his god. The altars were prepared for sacrifice, and the heads of the dead invaders and even their horses were set on the ceremonial poles by the temple of Huitzilopochtli. From out of the flayed man's eyes he saw the offering being brought to him along the wide streets lined with the thousands of the city of Mexico. To make certain there would be no unseemly display during the ceremony, the "messenger" had been forced to eat and drink a mixture made of sacred mushrooms and ground coca leaves.

Juan de Castro sweated beneath the ceremonial mask. His eyes dilated, he moved as if in a dream world. He had been sweating heavily even before he was given the mixture. He felt lightheaded and dizzy. Faces swam before him, and the feathered robe seemed very heavy. He moved in time with the beat of the drums that were covered with the skin of humans. Reed flutes shrieked above them, and in his drugged state he thought that he could hear the breathing of every one of the thousands on the streets. Slaves went before him, casting flowers to the crowd as naked girls swept the earth in front of him with their hair. He felt strangely content and at peace. Behind the mask he smiled at the painted faces around him. On either side priests, their faces painted black, helped to guide his steps as they began the climb to the top of the temple.

He stood, his back to the sacrificial stone, making no move or protest as his mask and robe were removed. His face had a pale waxy cast to it. Cuahtemoc motioned for him to step back. He did as he was commanded. It all seemed so natural. Even the man wearing another's skin did not seem out of place. Gentle hands helped him lie back on the darkly stained stone. It felt cool and pleasing to his hot flesh.

His arms were stretched out to the sides. Priests held them taut as they stretched out the skin of his chest and arched his back. Cuahtemoc stood over him as thousands of voices in the streets below chanted paeans to their gods, praying for this messenger to be accepted.

Cuahtemoc raised the knife of flint to the four winds. Drums and flutes increased the tempo to a crescendo. The knife plunged, sliced down, and was pulled to the side, exposing the chest cavity and the thing Cuahtemoc sought—Juan's beating heart. Grasping the pumping, rubbery organ in his hand, Cuahtemoc severed the arteries and muscles holding it. Juan never screamed. The pain he felt was a distant thing that had no relationship to him. There was only a vague discomfort as his mouth filled with blood and he died.

Cuahtemoc showed his prize to the people of Mexico, and they roared their approval. The new king was pleased at the way the ceremony had gone. To honor his victim, he had Juan's body sliced into thin strips and distributed to the mob, who ate the flesh as a sign of honor to the messenger.

Casca felt a stab of pain in his chest. It nearly doubled him over. He knew that pain well. Looking back at the great city, he thought he heard a distant rumble of voices crying out in righteous joy. He knew that Juan was gone. It was also time for him to leave this land of smoking mountains and death. He had failed, and there was no longer anything for him here.

That night he walked past the last sentry and went into the desert. Looking at the stars, he faced to the east and began to walk. He took with him his battered armor and sword and the small pouch of gems. With them he could arrange passage back to Cuba and from there take a ship to somewhere else he didn't belong; perhaps Peru or Africa.

That night the Aztecs rejoiced in their victory, not knowing that death more terrible than the guns of the Spaniards or even the knives of their priests was already walking among them. When they ate of the body of young Juan de Castro, they ate death. For in the cells of his fevered flesh he carried *smallpox* . . .